Cougar
Cove

Cougar Cove

JULIE LAWSON

ORCA BOOK PUBLISHERS

Canadian Cataloguing in Publication Data
Lawson, Julie, 1947 –
Cougar Cove
ISBN 1-55143-072-X
I. Title.
PS8573.A94C68 1996   jC813'.54   C95–911172–7
PZ7.L43828Co 1996

The publisher would like to acknowledge the ongoing
financial support of The Canada Council, the British
Columbia Ministry of Small Business, Tourism and Culture,
and the Department of Canadian Heritage.

Cover design by Christine Toller
Cover painting by David Powell
Interior illustrations by David Powell
Printed and bound in Canada

Orca Book Publishers
PO Box 5626, Station B
Victoria, BC V8R 6S4
Canada

Orca Book Publishers
PO Box 468
Custer, WA 98240-0468
USA

10 9 8 7 6 5 4 3

for Chris

Acknowledgements

This book started out as a picture book. I'm grateful to my editor, Ann Featherstone, who read that early version and suggested it might work better as a juvenile novel. Thanks, Ann, for helping me see the bigger picture.

My thanks to Bob Smirl, District Conservation Officer for Victoria, B.C., for sharing his knowledge and experience — and above all, his enthusiasm. He gave generously of his time and answered my questions with enormous patience. I'm also grateful to him for reading this book in manuscript form. His comments were helpful, and greatly appreciated.

To my dad and brother — the fishermen in my family — thanks for helping me sort out the herring strips and buzz bombs, and for sharing your fish stories. I'm grateful for your comments and suggestions.

Certain events described in *Cougar Cove* have actually happened. Others may well have happened, or could happen in the future. It is a work of fiction, however, and all the characters are fictitious.

The poem referred to in Chapter Ten is "Fog" by Carl Sandburg, first published in *Chicago Poems* by Henry Holt and Company, New York, 1916.

ONE

Getting There

I heard the cry of a cougar once and I won't forget it. Only once. Only for a moment. There were other sounds that summer. But that's the sound I remember.

There were pictures, too. Pictures of me rowing, fishing, roasting hot dogs, watching the great blue herons. I think I look happy.

The picture I remember most often, though, is the one in my mind. Even if I'd had a camera that day I couldn't have taken the picture. The click of the

1

shutter might have startled the cougar, and who knows what would have happened? But the picture stays with me. I won't forget it.

Sometimes, when my window is open, a breeze comes in and picks up the scent of that summer. It's in my seashells, in the pressed leaves of fern and cedar, in the dried bit of moss from the meadow. And with that smell I'm back in the woods that the cougars call home, where even a breath of wind carries the sea.

"Seatbelt fastened?"

Samantha Ross nodded to her aunt, then raised her arms so the flight attendant could see she was buckled in. But no matter how snugly the seatbelt fit, Sam couldn't buckle in her excitement. In five hours she'd be on the West Coast of Canada.

Mom jokingly called it "The Land of Fog." Sam liked the expression. It made the West Coast sound mysterious.

As the plane taxied down the runway, she opened her bag of Gummi Bears, a going-away present from her best friend, Angie. She popped a green one into her mouth, remembering how Angie's excitement had equalled her own.

"You mean you're really going OUT WEST?"

Angie had shrieked. "All the way to VANCOUVER?"

"No, Vancouver Island!" Sam helped herself to one of Angie's freshly cut orange quarters. "I'm flying to Vancouver first, then changing planes and flying to the island. Then my uncle Lon — "

"So it's an ISLAND? On the OCEAN?"

"What else?" Sam laughed. "That's why it's called Vancouver Island. And it's on the Pacific Ocean, and after my uncle meets us at the airport we're driving miles and miles to their house — "

"Your parents are going?"

"Nope, I'm going by myself. Well, with Auntie Jean. She's coming to Toronto for some teachers' conference and then she's taking me home with her."

"You're staying the whole summer?"

"Four weeks. I leave on July 15 and I'm staying until the middle of August. That's when Mom and Dad are coming to get me. And I've got two cousins, Alex and Robyn, and guess what? They're twins."

"And they live on the ocean?"

"Yup, their house is miles away from anywhere and it's right on the beach and there's woods all around — "

"You're so LUCKY! I'd kill to go to the ocean. Do they have a boat?"

"Nope, they've got *three!*"

"Oh, Sam." Angie slurped the juice from another orange quarter. "Wouldn't you rather stay in Toronto with me?"

"Definitely! When I think of all the sticky heat I'm going to miss — "

"Get out of here." Angie gave her a playful shove. "Will you write?"

"I'll be too busy having fun, but I'll try."

At the same moment, they had reached for an orange quarter, stuffed them into their mouths, and faced each other with huge orange peel grins.

Sam smiled at the memory, and helped herself to a yellow Gummi Bear. With her face glued to the window, she could see the runway rushing past as the plane gathered speed. Faster, faster — and with a whining shriek it was off the ground, wheels tucked under, nose aimed skyward. "Ohhh!" she gasped. For a moment her heart plummetted and she felt a touch of dizziness, but the feeling passed as the plane levelled off.

She concentrated on the scene below, a maze of highways, streets and houses. Many yards were studded with the turquoise of outdoor pools. I won't need a swimming pool this summer, she thought. I'll have the Pacific Ocean. Happily she reached for another Gummi Bear.

As well as Angie's going-away present, she had received presents from her parents. Mom gave her eight sheets of notepaper printed with cat's paws, four pre-stamped envelopes, and instructions to write one letter home each week. She also received a special pen. On the inside, the elevator of the landmark CN tower slid up and down, and on the outside, glittery letters spelled TORONTO. "So you won't forget where home is," Mom said, kissing Sam good-bye. "Have a good time, dear. And be careful you don't lean against the fog."

Sam laughed at her mother's familiar joke. "You mean the fog is *that* thick?"

"Partly." Mom gave her a hug. "But I don't want you counting on things too much. You know how carried away you get. Sometimes your expectations — "

"*Mom!*" Sam protested. "I don't really need a lecture, you know."

"All right. Fine. I don't want you to be hurt or disappointed, that's all."

"Don't worry! It's going to be perfect."

Dad gave her a book. Not a book for reading, but a book for writing — a shiny, hard-cover blank book. Not a plain one, either. The cover had a complicated design of leaves and petals, pale green and blue and peach, highlighted with flecks of gold. "A journal," Dad had called it.

Sam called it wonderful. As the plane settled into its cruising altitude, she pictured herself opening the book every night, turning to a creamy blank page, and writing about her day. She could write anything she wanted. She could write about Auntie Jean, Uncle Lon, and the twins. She could write about their home on Vancouver Island, about the ocean and mountains, about all the new things she would see and hear and taste and touch and feel. Best of all, she could write about her adventures in the mysterious Land of Fog. Everything she wrote would be wonderful. It was that kind of book.

Maybe she'd start by writing about how happy she was to be with her cousins. She had met them only once, five years earlier, when the whole Ross clan gathered in Toronto for a family reunion.

"I never knew we had so many relatives," nine-year-old Robyn exclaimed. "Did you, Sam-bone?"

Six-year-old Sam giggled. "I'm not a Sam-bone."

"I know. But you *are* my favourite cousin."

Sam grinned happily. Out of twenty-six cousins and second-cousins, Robyn was her favourite, too. She idolized her and her twin brother, Alex.

For the three days of endless eating and talking, Alex and Robyn adopted Sam. They took her exploring in their grandparents' garden, pushed her on swings in the nearby park, taught her Crazy Eights, and took turns reading her stories.

Sam cried when it was time for them to leave.

"You'll have to come to the coast for a holiday," Auntie Jean said when they were saying good-bye at the airport.

Sam's mother had smiled and said, "One of these days."

Finally, five years later, that day had arrived. With a contented sigh, Sam pressed her face against the window and watched Ontario disappear. Forests crept toward the prairie. Manitoba and Saskatchewan were taken up by lunch and a movie. Before she knew it, they were soaring over Alberta and the foothills of the Rockies. A short time later — "Look, Auntie Jean! The Rocky Mountains!" She printed on her mind every glacier, every lake, every snow-covered peak.

And then — "The ocean! Is that it, Auntie Jean? Is that really the ocean?"

"Sure is! We're almost there."

Shortly after the snack, the plane began its descent. "As soon as we get off," Auntie Jean said, "we've got to dash for our connecting flight. No time to see Vancouver, I'm afraid."

Sam didn't care. The sooner she got to the island, the sooner her adventure would begin.

TWO

A Bad Beginning

"Hi there, Samantha!" Uncle Lon's boisterous hug matched his voice. "How was your trip?"

Unexpectedly, Sam found herself tongue-tied. Did she know this person? Her uncle didn't look the same. He'd lost most of his hair since the reunion, his beard was grey, and he'd definitely put on a few pounds.

"Must feel kind of strange, eh? Leaving the big city and coming all this way. But just you wait," he

boomed. "After a couple of days you'll feel like a real West Coaster."

"Sam-bone! Is it really you?" Sam turned to see a tall, lanky girl pushing her way toward the arrival gate. "You're such a shrimp. I thought you'd be way bigger by now."

Sam gave the girl a blank look.

"I'm Robyn! Don't you remember your own cousin?" She rolled her eyes in a gesture of annoyance.

Sam gave her a shy smile. What she remembered was a nine-year-old Robyn. She had not pictured this leggy, fourteen-year-old teenager. And if Robyn had changed so much, what would Alex be like? Since they were twins, he'd still have Robyn's colouring and features, right down to the same lopsided grin. But he was a boy. How tall would *he* be? What would his voice be like? And his attitude? For the first time, she heard a small inner voice saying, Maybe Mom was right ...

Uncle Lon picked up the luggage and led the way to the parking lot. "We've got a long drive ahead of us," he said. "Anybody hungry? Thirsty? Need a pit stop?"

"Not this little red duck," said Auntie Jean. "I just want to get home. How about you, Sam?"

Sam shook her head. Pit stop? Red duck? Who *were* these people?

"Alex is making supper," Robyn said as they drove off. "Can you believe it, Mom? Something fishy. Sockeye surprise or abalone rigatoni." She turned to

Sam. "No matter how awful it tastes, pretend you like it. Alex has very fragile feelings."

Uncle Lon burst out laughing. "And the sun sets in the east."

"No it doesn't," Sam found herself saying. "It sets in the west."

Robyn gave her a surprised look. "Does it really? I didn't think things were that different in Toronto."

Sam frowned. "It's not just Toronto."

"Robyn's teasing," said Auntie Jean. "Don't pay any attention."

"Are you always so gullible, Sam-bone?"

"Robyn, that's enough. Sam's had a long trip and she's tired. It's eight o'clock Toronto time, don't forget. Almost bedtime." She stifled a yawn. "We've both got a serious case of jet lag, don't you think, Sam? But never mind. You'll get used to it, the time change and all."

"I've got a book you'd like," Robyn continued. "It's called *Gullible's Travels*. Have you read it?"

"Uh-huh," Sam said sleepily. She was beginning to feel terribly small, like Gullible — no, Gulliver — when he was in Brobding-something, the Land of the Giants. But Gulliver spent time in the Land of the Little People, too. He was a giant amongst the Lilliputians. Maybe she'd have her turn as the giant. She'd been such a good one in the school play ...

Robyn leaned over and whispered, "Our house is a bit rustic, but you'll get used to it. Especially the outhouse."

Sam gulped. Outhouse?

They drove off the highway onto another road that took them past car lots and gas stations and the same fast food restaurants she knew from home. Before long they were on a country road, winding through trees bigger and greener than any Sam had seen.

"How's your stomach?" Uncle Lon asked. "This road is pretty twisty."

Sam hadn't noticed until he mentioned it. But now her stomach was definitely protesting. A short time ago they had turned onto a narrow road with the ups and downs and twists and turns of a roller coaster. Uncle Lon's sudden swerves to avoid potholes didn't help. "Uhhh," she groaned.

"Not much farther," Uncle Lon said heartily. "We'll do the guided tour bit — keep your mind off your stomach. See to your right? That big puddle is the basin. Looks like a lake, doesn't it? The road follows it all the way around, then veers off along the harbour and dead ends at the strait. That's our neck of the woods, right next to a wilderness park."

"Uhhh … " Sam rolled down the window, stuck her head out and took big gulps of air. Please don't let me be carsick, she prayed. Please …

"How about trading places?" Auntie Jean suggested. "It's always worse in the back seat."

When Uncle Lon stopped the car, Sam stumbled out and moved shakily into the front.

"Any better?" Auntie Jean asked after awhile.

Sam took another gulp of air. "Uh-huh."

"I used to be carsick all the time," said Robyn. "Remember, Mom? We could never go on this road without a barf bag. Remember that time I ate all those cherries? And we — "

"Stop!" Sam yelled. She leaped out of the car and threw up in the ditch.

Auntie Jean handed her a Kleenex. "Almost there, honey."

"Could I walk the rest of the way?"

Robyn hooted with laughter. "It's forever!"

"We'll take it slower," Uncle Lon said. "That'll help."

"Feels better once you've barfed, though," said Robyn. "Doesn't it?"

Sam didn't answer.

Moments later, Sam woke with a start. "What's that sound?"

"Our resident foghorn," her uncle said. "It bellows from a lighthouse directly across from our place. But don't worry, you'll get used to it."

Sam stared out the window, amazed. Mom hadn't been kidding. It really was the Land of Fog. She had dozed off for ten, maybe fifteen minutes, but in that short time they had left the sun and entered a world of white. She could see trees at the sides of the road or directly ahead, but the rest of the world was gone.

Soon they stopped before a large wooden sign, carved with the words *Brackenwood Point*. "Home sweet home," Robyn said as she hopped out to open the gate.

Sam was about to follow when her aunt said, "Sit tight, we've still got a ways to go. But we're getting closer all the time."

"Whew," Sam sighed. The driveway wound through acres of woods that floated in and out of the fog. It really was mysterious. A person could get lost and never be found. And what strange creatures might be lurking? She shivered, as if a clammy finger of fog had touched the back of her neck.

Finally the car came to a stop. "We made it!" Auntie Jean gestured to a sprawling cedar shingle house perched like a lookout at the end of the point. "Here it is, Sam. Welcome to Brackenwood."

Sam scrambled out, eager to stretch her muscles. She hadn't taken two steps when she stopped, wrinkling her nose. "Eugh! What's that smell?"

"My putrid brother," said Robyn.

Auntie Jean shook her head. "Honestly, that kid. It's low tide, Sam."

"Sea and salt and seaweed and clams," a deep voice said behind her. "Not to mention mud and guck and dead fish. Hi, Sam. How's *Trawna?*"

Sam looked up at the tall, thin stranger she figured was Alex and said, "Fine, I guess." It seemed as if she'd left Toronto months ago.

"What do you want to do first? Eat some of my gourmet straight-out-of-the-package frozen fish sticks? Turn off the foghorn? Go fishing for kelp? See the runabout and check out the outboard?"

Runabout? Outboard?

Uncle Lon laughed at her confused expression. "A type of boat and a motor. Don't worry, you'll get used to all these new words."

You'll get used to it. How many times had she heard that expression? And would she *ever* get used to it?

Alex must have read her mind. "You better," he said. "There's going to be a test, and if you fail, you can't get off the island. So what do you want to do?"

"She wants to see her room, have supper and go to sleep," Auntie Jean said. "The pair of us are bushed."

Sam smiled gratefully. Her adventure hadn't started the way she'd imagined. The sooner tomorrow arrived, the better.

THREE

Disaster

"Well, Sam, what do you think?" Uncle Lon grinned as the *Misty Jean* sped away from the dock. "Isn't this the life? Sure beats muggy Toronto."

Sam breathed in the tangy sea air and nodded happily. The night before, her uncle had promised to take her fishing — provided she could get up before dawn. Since 3:30 that morning, she'd been awake and waiting.

Robyn sprawled across the seat in the cabin

cruiser and yawned noisily. "How did you do it, Sambone? I'm half-asleep."

"Guess I'm still on Toronto time."

"You'll be on Pacific time before you know it," her uncle said. "Boy, what a day! Just look at that water. Not a ripple."

"That's why it's called the Pacific, right?" said Sam. "My teacher told us it's Spanish for peaceful."

"Would've had a whole different name if that explorer — who was he again? — had first seen it during a storm."

The sky was still dark as he steered the boat around the spit. Pointing up to the lighthouse, he said, "There's the foghorn, quiet for once. It's going to be a great day."

Sam agreed. In her mind, she was already writing the first entry in her journal. *Early this morning, when the stars were still out, I went fishing. For the very first time! In the Pacific Ocean! It was wonderful!*

Once around the spit, the boat zoomed off into the strait, leaving a trail of silver. An island rose in the distance, lit by the first pale wash of dawn. As he approached the island, Uncle Lon slowed the engine to a trolling speed. "Good a spot as any," he said, taking out the fishing tackle.

"How do you know?" Sam wondered.

He winked. "Feel it in my bones."

"Meaning, we'll be as unlucky here as anywhere else," Robyn said.

"Oh, go on. Now, how about the rods? Alex,

you've got yours, Robyn — "

"Sam can use mine. Do you want to?"

"Sure!" Sam beamed at her cousin.

"That leaves mine," Uncle Lon said. "Three ought to do it. Now, how about rigging up these strip teasers?"

"Not me," said Alex. "I'm using a hoochie."

"Hoochie-koochie," Robyn teased, twirling a rubbery orange squid in his face. "You want a hoochie, Sam?"

Sam shrugged. "Whatever … "

"Nah, I'll give you the good old reliable strip teaser. It's really a herring strip, and you put it inside this plastic holder thing, OK? Like I'm doing for Dad. Salmon love herring."

Sam watched Robyn, then attached her own, grimacing at the slimy feel of the herring. But if this is the way West Coasters do it, she told herself, this is the way I'll do it. When the herring strip was in place, Robyn helped her tie on a weight, then showed her how to let out the line. "Keep going … "

"To the bottom?"

"Not that far. We're not fishing for cod, at least not today."

When the line was out far enough, Uncle Lon secured the rod to the edge of the boat. "Now all you have to do is wait. As soon as that little bell rings, start to reel her in."

"You won't need the bell," Alex said. "The rod will be thumping like crazy."

Sam waited patiently. But after admiring the sunrise, eating three blueberry muffins, and drinking a cup of cocoa from Robyn's thermos, she began to wish something would happen.

Robyn read her mind. "Boring, huh?"

Sam gave the rod a shake. "When will they start to bite?"

"As soon as your mind is on something else," her uncle said. "Think about how smart fish are."

"Smart?"

"They swim around in schools, don't they?"

Sam giggled, while her cousins groaned.

"Old joke, Dad," said Alex. "Did you hear the one about — "

"Sam, you've got one!" Robyn let out a sudden whoop. "Grab the reel, quick!"

"It's heavy!" Sam clung to the rod, dizzy with excitement. "I can hardly — "

"Want some help?"

"No way!" She tightened her grip and turned the reel as the rod tugged and bucked in her hand.

"That's the way!" Uncle Lon said. "Give the line some slack so it doesn't snap. Keep going!"

Just then, the fish appeared, slapping its tail against the surface of the water. Silvery-blue scales glistened in the sun. "Wow!" Sam exclaimed. "Is that a salmon?"

"Yeah!" Robyn cheered. "Way to go, Sam-bone!"

"Atta girl!" said Uncle Lon. "You're doing fine!"

Each turn of the reel brought the fish closer. But the closer it got, the more Sam wondered — did she really want to bring it in? Or did she want to set it free?

All of a sudden Alex hollered from behind. "Dad! Your line — holy jeez — I've got one, too!"

Uncle Lon leaped to his rod. As Sam glanced over her shoulder to see how he and Alex were doing, her fish gave a tremendous tug and whipped the rod right out of her hands.

"GET IT!" Robyn lunged over the side in a desperate attempt to grab her rod, but it had already disappeared. "Sam! How could you let go like that? Why didn't you hold on?"

"I — I tried!" Sam stammered, fighting to hold back the tears. "I didn't mean to — "

"Robyn, quick!" Alex cried. "Pass me the net and the fish club!" He grabbed the net and scooped his catch out of the water. Then he took the club and whacked the fish on the head. "Three-pound coho, looks like. What a beaut, eh, Sam?"

She bit her lip and winced at the sight of the lifeless fish. "I'm sorry, I — "

"Don't worry about it. I got this one and Dad's got his, see? And there's still time for more bites."

Sam sniffed noisily. "But the rod! I lost — "

"Fishing's like that." Uncle Lon patted her shoulder. "Believe me, that's not the first rod that got away."

Sam looked at Robyn, slumped inside the cabin. "But Robyn — "

"She'll get over it. That rod needed replacing, anyway."

"I can buy her a new one. I've got some money."

"Forget it." He finished letting out his line and said, "How about keeping an eye on my rod? She's all ready to go."

While he went to talk to Robyn, Sam stared at his rod, praying that the next fish would pick Alex's line.

"Four coho!" Auntie Jean greeted them on the dock with her camera. "Congratulations! This demands a picture."

They stood by the boat and faced the camera, each holding a fish. "Everybody ready? One, two — C'mon, Robyn. Smile."

Robyn snarled under her breath and mumbled something Sam couldn't hear.

"OK, here we go. Say cheese!"

"Say disaster," Robyn muttered.

Auntie Jean clicked the shutter. "One more, to be sure."

Sam dutifully said "cheese" but her smile felt sticky, as if it were glued with melted mozzarella. So much for writing this day in my journal, she thought. So much for wonderful.

On the other hand, the day wasn't over.

FOUR

How Can You Be So Stupid?

"Ready for the tour?" Robyn asked. "We're leaving in two minutes." Sometime during lunch, between the crab sandwiches and raspberry sherbet, she had cast off her glum mood and decided to take Sam exploring.

Alex joined them outside. "Hope you've got your survival gear," he said as they started out. "Did Robyn tell you?"

Sam gave her cousin a worried look. "How far are we going?"

"Gotcha!" Robyn laughed. "You fall for everything."

Sam smiled. At least Robyn was speaking to her again.

The tour started on the beach. As they walked along, Sam could see that Brackenwood Point was almost completely surrounded by water. Each side had a sheltered bay. Directly across was a small village, to the right was the harbour that led into the basin, and to the left was the spit. Beyond the spit was the strait that separated Vancouver Island from the United States.

"Don't forget there's a test," Alex said for the millionth time.

Sam hadn't forgotten. In her mind she chanted the names she'd heard earlier that morning: Juan de Fuca Strait, Olympic Mountains, Washington. Before long, they were snarled up in the other names Alex kept throwing at her. "Mussel, limpet, barnacle, cockleshell — "

"OK, OK!" she said in frustration. Her head was beginning to feel like a tidepool. She wouldn't remember a thing if he didn't stop hammering at her.

Somewhere between the limpets and barnacles they left the rocky beach and entered the woods. "We've got thirty-two acres," Alex said proudly, "and right next door is a wilderness park. Over three thousand acres or 1,422 hectares, if you want to think metric."

"I think huge," said Sam. Trails crisscrossed through stands of cedar, fir and hemlock, red alder

24

and maple. Years ago, the property had been logged. Massive stumps remained, almost hidden by clumps of salal, Oregon grape and ferns, and the flowers of ocean spray, once white, now dried to the colour of tobacco. "What were those for?" she asked, pointing to notches cut in one enormous stump.

"Springboards," Alex explained. "Loggers cut out the notches, stuck in the springboards, then stood on them, one on either side. They used a hand saw — a real long one — to cut down the tree. One logger on each end. No chain saws in those days."

Sam paused to examine a seedling growing out of the stump. The needles were about one inch long, and stuck out from the twigs in all directions, like bristles on a bottle brush. "That's a Douglas fir, right?"

"Hey! Fast learner," said Robyn. "And this bush with the red berries is a huckleberry. Try some, they're poisonous. Just kidding," she added, popping one into her mouth. "They're quite good if you like sour."

They ate a few tart berries, then continued along the path until they came to a fork. "The path to the right is a shortcut to the Duncans' place next door," Alex said. "They've got a farm."

"With killer sheep," said Robyn.

"Really?" Sam's eyes grew wide.

"Gotcha again, Gullible! No, seriously. They've got a ram that butted Alex once, smack in the bum. He couldn't sit down for weeks. Could you, butt-head?"

Alex ignored her. "If you keep going straight, the

path leads into the park. But first it goes over a creek."

"Don't ever drink the water," Robyn cut in, "unless you're dying of thirst. Or unless you like the taste of skunk cabbage."

"And if you go to the left, like we're doing now, you end up back at the house. Unless you make a right up here and keep going until you get to the driveway, which will take you out to the road." He gave Sam a mischievous grin. "Have you got all that? Don't forget — "

"There's a test," she sighed. "I know." It was very confusing. Would she ever find her way around these woods? Now Alex was turning down another path, lined with fragrant orange honeysuckle. Where does *this* one go? she wondered.

A curve in the path led them to a small shingled structure painted dark green to blend in with the trees. "Ta-daa!" Robyn opened the door with a flourish. Inside was a wooden bench with a hole, a roll of toilet paper, whitewashed walls, and a bucket of clamshells. There was also a box of crayons. "That's your job, Sam-bone. Everyone who stays here has to colour shells to decorate the outhouse."

"How many?"

"You're here for four weeks. How about one a day? Seven times four, that makes — "

"Twenty-eight."

"Very good! By the way, did Mom tell you about the problem with the septic tank? You can't use the inside plumbing at night. You have to use the outhouse. Don't worry, I'll leave a flashlight in your room."

"The bears don't come till blackberry season," Alex said.

"When's that?"

"Middle of August, usually."

"But you can't always count on it," Robyn said. "Bears are very unpredictable."

"Unlike squirrels," said Alex. "Do you want to feed our squirrel when we get back?"

"Or go to the village with Mom and me?" Robyn raised her eyebrows expectantly.

Sam looked from one to the other, wondering what to do. "Feed the squirrel," she said, finally. Robyn's mood could change. But what could go wrong, feeding a squirrel?

Later in the afternoon, Alex called Sam to the kitchen window. "There he is. See, on that cedar branch?"

Sam looked up and saw one branch dip, another one sway. "Where — ? Oh!" The squirrel scampered along the branch, then leaped across to another tree. From cedar to fir he went, until he reached a branch that led straight to the railing of the deck.

"He's really fussy," Alex said, handing her a large bag of peanuts. "He'll only eat them if they're shelled properly. Sometimes he'll eat right out of your hand."

"I'll do it properly, don't worry." She and Angie had often fed squirrels in the parks and ravines of Toronto, but they were ordinary city squirrels, not special like this grey one. Imagine, a wild West Coast squirrel, so friendly and tame he would eat out of her hand, right beside the Pacific Ocean. *That* was how she'd begin her journal.

Her appearance on the deck startled the squirrel, and with a flick of his bushy tail, he scampered into the treetops. "You'll be back," she called.

By the time Auntie Jean and Robyn returned from the village she had shelled every peanut and stacked them in neat piles along the railing. "Guess what!" she exclaimed. "Alex said the squirrel would eat out of my hand if I — "

"*What?*" Robyn stared in disbelief.

"Shelled the peanuts. Alex said — "

"He was kidding, Gullible. Squirrels crack the shells themselves. Everybody knows that."

"I know, but … " She felt herself shrink. "I thought they might be different here."

Robyn rolled her eyes and gave Sam a withering look. "How can you be so *stupid?* Like — "

"Robyn!" Auntie Jean spoke sharply.

Sam tried to laugh it off. "Yeah, it was pretty stupid." With a shrug she retreated to her room.

From behind the closed door she could hear her aunt's angry voice. "I know you're upset about Kate going away but that's no reason to make everyone else miserable."

"*Mom!* She lost my fishing rod, how am I supposed to feel? Elated?"

"She's only just arrived. She's bound to feel a bit out of place."

"I didn't do anything!"

"It wouldn't kill you to be pleasant. She wants you to like her. Why can't you — "

"Alex was the one who told her to shell the flipping peanuts. You take everything out on me. It's not fair!"

Sam heard her aunt speak again, too quietly to make out the words. Then Robyn loudly protested, "Why does she take everything so seriously? Doesn't she know we're kidding? How can she be so stupid?"

Back to the beginning. Sam flung herself face down on the bed and covered her ears. Her eyes welled up with tears. Auntie Jean was right. She *did* want her cousins to like her. But so far, everything she'd done had turned out to be wrong or stupid. And this was only the first day. How would she get through the remaining twenty-seven?

Her worries were interrupted by a shout from the beach. "Robyn, hurry up! The motor's running and I promised we'd get to the wharf by four o'clock."

Good, Sam thought. They're leaving.

But Robyn was still on the deck when she went outside. "I was just going to call you. Want to come with us? We're meeting some friends at Fisherman's Wharf."

Sam shook her head, knowing the invitation had not been her cousin's idea.

"Too bad," Robyn said, and bolted off to join her brother. Sam couldn't help but notice how relieved she looked.

Well, fine. She would sit here on the deck and wait for the squirrel. He'd eat the peanuts anyway, wouldn't he? She might as well, too.

As she sat munching the peanuts, a blacktail deer stepped out of the woods, crossed the lawn and paused to nibble the orange and yellow nasturtiums. Sam smiled, enjoying the idea of snacking along with the deer. But her pleasure was short-lived.

"Go on, you beast! Shoo!" Auntie Jean streaked across the yard, waving a windbreaker around her head. "Out, out!"

The deer leaped to the edge of the lawn, then stopped. Glancing over its shoulder as if to say, "I know you don't really mean it," it bit a leaf off the rhododendron and, chewing thoughtfully, faced Auntie Jean.

"I'm not kidding!" she yelled, running toward the deer. "Get lost!"

The deer bounded over the ferns and disappeared.

"I'll give her two minutes," Auntie Jean said. "You'll see, she'll be back. Every year it's the same thing. I finally figure out what flowers they *don't* like, then they go and develop a taste for them. One of these days I'm going to develop a taste for venison."

"You wouldn't!" Sam gave her aunt a horrified look.

"No," Auntie Jean laughed. "Probably not. See, what did I tell you? Here she comes, bold as brass."

She took a handful of peanuts and sat beside Sam. "What are you doing here all by yourself? Didn't you want to go in the boat?"

"Maybe later."

"Don't let the twins bother you. They're very close, closer than any brothers and sisters I've ever known. Guess they've had to be. We're so isolated here, they've always relied on each other. As for Robyn, it's her nature to blow hot and cold, so don't take it personally."

"I thought I heard — did her best friend move away?"

"Only for the summer. I guess that's part of it, although she has other friends in the village. But she's very egocentric, our Robyn. Hates to think that anyone might be getting more attention than she is. Even her little cousin." She gave Sam a pat on the knee. "She feels like you've invaded her territory, and she's a bit jealous. But don't worry, she'll get used to you. Give it some time."

Sam swallowed hard. I don't want more time, she wanted to say. I want to go home.

An angry chittering caused her to look up and see the squirrel, peering down from a branch. "You want the rest of these? Come on, then."

But the squirrel, like Robyn, wanted her gone. It wasn't until she left the deck that he came to eat the remaining peanuts. Watching him through the kitchen window, she felt as if she'd already been given Alex's test. And already, she'd failed.

FIVE

More Worries

"Fresh salmon for dinner!" Uncle Lon announced. "Can't beat that, eh, Sam?"

"Watch out for bones," Alex said. "There could be a few, just waiting for an unsuspecting gullet. Keep some bread handy, just in case."

Sam placed another dinner roll on her plate. All she needed was a bone stuck in her throat. Choking to death in front of her cousins was not how she wanted to be remembered.

"How old are you now, Sam?" Uncle Lon asked, passing the salad. "I can't keep track anymore."

"I just turned eleven, on July 10."

"Eleven?" Robyn's jaw dropped. "You look more like nine."

Sam swallowed too quickly and panicked. Was that sharp scratching against the back of her throat a bone? Couldn't be. A piece of celery from the salad, that's all. Relieved, she cleared her throat and said, "I can't help it if I'm small."

"Good things come in small packages," said Uncle Lon.

Robyn smirked. "Yeah, Dad. Like poison and black widow spiders."

Auntie Jean changed the subject. "What do you like best about school?"

"Drama!" This was a favourite topic, and a safe one. "I've been in every school play and this year I was the giant in *Jack and the Beanstalk.*"

"You? A giant?" Alex laughed. "They must have been hard up."

"Size didn't matter. I wore a giant's costume with a big papier-mâché head. The shoulders were held up by poles attached to a backpack. My eyes looked out of the belt buckle. I had a pole to make the mouth open and close and I spoke through a microphone. I got to be the giant because I've got a loud voice." She helped herself to more salad, pleased that she'd been able to string more than two sentences together. "Once for Halloween I was the Lion King. And I roared so loudly my cat Rupert got scared and took off for a week."

"You're full of surprises," Uncle Lon said with a grin. "Just like your mom. When we were kids she used to scare the socks off me with her bellow. Such a little squirt, too."

Robyn leaned across the table. "Do it. Do your loud giant voice. Or your roar."

Sam's throat squeezed up like an accordion. Was it a bone this time? Frantic, she tore off a chunk of her dinner roll and swallowed.

"Well?" Robyn persisted.

Sam drank some milk to wash down the roll. Whew! Nothing was stuck in her throat. But no matter how much she wanted to bellow out *Fee Foe Fie Fum*, she couldn't. "I can be loud if I want to be," she said. "I just don't feel like it now."

"Yeah, right." Robyn gave her a look that said, We knew you couldn't do it.

Sam wished she could climb up a beanstalk and disappear.

There was blackberry pie for dessert. "The last of last summer's berries," Auntie Jean said. "We'll have to start picking pretty soon, and stock up the freezer."

"We saw a bear last year," Robyn said. "Labour Day weekend. One day we were picking blackberries, and the next day there was the bear, right in the exact same spot."

"Is that true?" Sam appealed to her aunt, hoping

she'd say Robyn was kidding.

Instead, Auntie Jean got up from the table and came back with a photograph album. "Not only true," she said, flipping through the pages, "but we've got proof positive. See?"

Sam stared at the photo of a black bear lounging in front of the blackberry bushes.

"He didn't stay long. After I took this picture he ambled off toward the Duncans' next door. See? There he is in the orchard, knocking down apples."

Sam forced down a mouthful of pie. "They don't come till August?"

"Nope," said Uncle Lon, "not till black bear-y season."

Auntie Jean smiled kindly. "Don't worry, Sam. In all the years we've been here, last year was the only time we ever saw a bear. They keep their distance."

"But you better be on the lookout, just in case."

"Stop it, Robyn. You're scaring her."

"Sorry, Gullible. Just kidding."

Maybe, Sam thought. But the pictures are real.

SIX

Sleepless Nights

Sam couldn't sleep. First, there was the worry. Before going to bed, Robyn had handed her a flashlight and whispered, "Don't forget — outhouse rules after lights out. And if you hear a scratching in the middle of the night, it's only the ghost in the attic. Unless it's the bear."

Second, there was the quiet. Where was the familiar sound of traffic? The hum of streetlights? Where was the *light?* It had been easy to fall asleep last night. Jet lag had seen to that. But now …

She turned her pillow to the cool side, curled up and tried counting sheep. It didn't work.

Maybe if she counted the worries. One the bear, two the ghost, three the outhouse, four the fishing rod, five tomorrow, six the day after, seven … Her heart began to thump, and she realized that counting worries was only making her more awake.

She remembered a listening exercise from school. Concentrate on sounds outside the room, then inside the room, then inside yourself. Maybe by then she'd be asleep.

She strained to listen for outside sounds, but silence drummed in her ears. No, wait —

Frogs! A whole clamouring chorus of them. From the creek? No, closer than that. Tree frogs, then. Auntie Jean had shown her the little frog that lived in the hanging basket by the front door. Sam smiled, remembering how it had hopped out when her aunt had watered the petunias, then hopped back, hiding under a dripping pink petal.

Concentrate! she told herself. Or you'll never get to sleep.

OK, forget the frogs. Listen for sounds inside the room. One, breathe in, two, breathe out … No, wait. Breathing counts as inside yourself. Listen, listen …

Then she heard it. A scratching above her head.

She turned on the flashlight and shone it at the wooden beam crossing the ceiling. The scratching stopped.

As soon as she turned off the light, the scratching started again. Louder, this time. Like a waterfall. Like a thousand fingernails trying to claw their way out. Or in.

Sam shuddered.

Robyn wasn't kidding.

It had to be a ghost.

But *whose* ghost? This wasn't an old haunted house kind of place. Her aunt and uncle had built it themselves, twenty years ago. No other family had lived here. No one had *died* here. At least, no one Sam knew about. Unless, unless …

What if her cousins had played some "just kidding" trick on some poor little kid and accidentally locked him — or her — in the attic? And then forgot all about him? Until it was too late? And what if —

Stop it! She gritted her teeth, clamped her hands over her ears and made herself think of Angie. What would she say? Something like, "A GHOST? You think you're in the middle of some *horror* story? Get out of here!" Then she'd laugh and nudge Sam playfully, before going off to make a sandwich.

The thought of down-to-earth, sensible Angie gave Sam a boost. Once again, she shone the flashlight at the beam. There wasn't an attic, she realized. So there couldn't have been a person up there. But a ghost? A ghost could come from anywhere. A ghost could *go* anywhere. A ghost could slip into the tiniest crack, even into that knot hole in the beam …

Sam thought her heart would burst from the

thumping. What should she do? Get up and tell her aunt? Go into Robyn's room? Yell? Roar?

She burrowed under the covers, so that only the tip of her nose was visible. Some giant she turned out to be.

Now it seemed as if the scratching was above the door and under the bed and along the window sill. Not one ghost but hundreds, in her head and under her skin, scratching away at the counting of worries, the counting of the endless days she had to endure before she could go home ...

"Morning, Sam! How did you sleep? Like a log, I bet, with all this sea air."

"I heard it, Auntie Jean."

"Oh, dear. I'm sorry. We should have — Hang on a sec, I'm expecting that call." She broke off to answer the phone.

"You heard the sea air?" said Alex, passing her the pancake syrup. "What was it, high C, low C or middle C?"

"The ghost." She went on to explain the mysterious scratching that had kept her awake.

"Told you!" Robyn crowed. "Don't worry, he's a friendly ghost. We call him Clarence."

"Don't listen to her," Alex said. "That scratching

sound is only carpenter ants. Dad said to tell you he's going to spray them. Otherwise they'll total the place. Did you see any saws coming through the beam? That's why they're called carpenter ants."

"For heaven's sake," his mother said, returning from the phone. "Don't you and Robyn ever stop? Sam, we have to apologize. Lon meant to get at those beastly ants before you got here, but it slipped his mind till last night. We heard them, too. One of the hazards of country living, I'm afraid. But they'll be gone by tomorrow."

So. Nothing but carpenter ants. Sam hadn't seen saws. But when she returned to her room she did notice a pile of sawdust on the floor beside the bed.

That night, since Sam's room had been sprayed, she had to sleep with Robyn. "Don't toss and turn, don't talk in your sleep, don't snore and don't sleepwalk."

"I never do," said Sam.

"And if you're having a good dream wake me up so I can be in it."

"Huh?"

"Never mind. Nothing wakes me up. Maybe an earthquake, but I haven't had that experience. G'night." She switched off the lamp, yawned noisily, and rolled over.

Sam lay there, trying to sleep. She tried counting sheep, but was no more successful than she'd been the night before. Outside sounds, inside sounds … She tried to concentrate. But all she could hear was one huge worry.

She had to go to the bathroom. Desperately.

And since the septic tank didn't work after lights out, she had to go to the outhouse.

In the woods. In the dark. Alone.

Not *exactly* in the dark, she told herself when she couldn't wait any longer. The moon was bright, she had her flashlight, and since she'd spent the afternoon colouring shells and arranging them on the outhouse bench, she knew the way. And how scary could it be? It wasn't *that* far from the house.

And there were no ghosts. At least that worry was gone. Talk about an overactive imagination.

Across the lawn, past the woodshed, second turn to the left … Cheered on by the tree frogs, she followed the path until it curved into the scent of honeysuckle. From there, she could see the outhouse with its crescent moon window. Relief was close at hand.

She sat there long after she needed to, with the

flashlight off and the door wide open. It'll be better from now on, she thought as she rearranged the clamshells. She hadn't done anything wrong or stupid since the squirrel. She *had* fallen for Robyn's ghost story, but that didn't really count. Anyway, Robyn would be pleased about the twenty-eight shells she'd coloured. And she hadn't woken her up to go to the outhouse, even though she had been scared.

Whoo-who-who-who-whooo

Her nerves tingled. An owl! What could be more wonderful, more adventurous than hearing an owl in the woods in the moonlight? Excited, she hurried outside and ran along the path.

Whoo-who-who-who-whooo

Maybe she'd see it! She'd sit on the deck for awhile and look into the treetops. Maybe take the quilt outside so she wouldn't get cold.

A rustling sound in the bushes made her run faster. Nervously, she glanced over her shoulder. Not watching where she was going, she ran smack into —

"Ooff!"

"Ow!" yelled a familiar voice.

"Ohh!" Sam gasped. "Uncle Lon!"

"Gosh, Sam! My stomach will never be the same. What are you doing here, this time of night? Couldn't you sleep?"

"I had to — Robyn said we had to use the outhouse at night and then I heard — "

"Robyn said *what?*"

As they walked back to the house, Sam told him.

"And I heard the owl! Did you, Uncle Lon?"

He nodded. "There'll be a few anxious rodents tonight. And how about you?" he asked as they stepped inside. "Think you can sleep?"

"I guess … "

"There's no need for you to be anxious. You don't have to go outside. That outhouse hasn't been used for years. That's why you can still smell the honeysuckle."

"Oh." Sam pushed her face into a smile. After saying good night, she crept back to bed, being extra careful not to disturb Robyn. She could hear it already. *How can you be so stupid?*

SEVEN

Jigging for Cod

"Robyn, there's fun teasing and there's just plain mean. You've crossed the line."

"Come on, Dad. I didn't think she'd really believe me. If she'd woken me up I would've told her."

"From now on — "

"Why can't she take a joke? And how come you always blame me? Like it's my fault she doesn't have a sense of humour."

"Robyn, you've got to … " Their voices faded away,

lost in the morning clatter of dishes and cutlery.

Sam stood behind the closed door, wishing she hadn't overheard. A few moments later, she heard her uncle say, "See you later." The car door slammed. The tea kettle started to whistle. She waited until she heard the water being poured, then took a deep breath and walked into the kitchen.

"Hi, Sam-bone," said Alex. "Or is it Lazy-bones? I hear the owl kept you awake."

Sam nodded. Anything she said was bound to be attacked by Robyn as wrong or stupid, so she decided it was best to keep quiet. Day three, she thought glumly as she sat down for breakfast. Twenty-five days left to go. Three whole weeks and four days. Times twenty-four hours a day ... She swallowed a mouthful of toast to stifle what felt like a sob.

"What's on the menu this morning?" said Auntie Jean.

"Looks like burnt toast to me," Robyn grumbled.

Her mother gave an exasperated sigh. "You know what I mean."

"Jigging for cod, Mom," said Alex. "We already told you."

Auntie Jean poured Sam a glass of orange juice. "You haven't been in the runabout yet, have you, Sam?"

Robyn glared at her mother. "There's just room for two of us." Turning to Sam she said, "You don't mind, do you? We can go later."

Sam looked down at her plate and swept the crumbs with her finger. "It's OK. I don't have to go."

"There's plenty of room." Auntie Jean gave Robyn a look that indicated the subject was closed

"Great." Robyn pushed back her chair and stomped out of the kitchen.

"It's really all right," Sam said, appealing to Alex.

"Don't pay any attention to her," he said. "Come on, the fish are waiting."

His friendly, lopsided grin raised Sam's spirits enormously. She finished her toast in three bites and washed it down with orange juice. Things wouldn't be so bad with Alex on her side.

Auntie Jean waved them off. "Bring me back a big one! I'm counting on grilled cod for supper, with hollandaise sauce."

And I'm counting on a wonderful day, Sam said to herself as she ran to catch up with her cousins. Anyone who heard an owl in the night had to be a new person the next morning. So what if Robyn was in a grouchy mood? Today, she would start writing in her journal. Because today, everything would be wonderful.

She couldn't have been more wrong.

"Not there!" Robyn snapped as Sam stepped into the runabout. "That's where Alex sits. Unless you're planning to run the boat," she added sarcastically.

Sam winced, and scooted to the seat in the middle.

"And that's my place. You can't sit there."

"Where, then? Up front?"

"Yes. And it's called a bow. There's a test, remember?"

Sam seated herself in the bow and sighed. Would they ever let her forget?

"Everybody ready?" Alex lowered the nine-horsepower outboard and jerked the starter cord. After three pulls, the engine roared to life. Soon they were at full throttle, speeding away from the dock. "Bombs away!" he exclaimed as they skimmed over the water.

"Buzz bombs, you mean," Robyn quipped. "Number fours, guaranteed to fool even the most intelligent of rockfish."

"An exceedingly rare and endangered species," said her brother.

"They're endangered?" Sam had to shout to make herself heard.

"You better hope the cod patrol isn't around," Robyn said. "It's a life sentence if you're caught."

Alex laughed at the worried expression on Sam's face. "She's kidding, Gullible. I said *intelligent* rockfish were endangered, not rockfish in general."

"I thought we were fishing for cod."

"Duh!" Robyn threw up her hands, exasperated. "What do you think cod are?"

"They're related to rockfish," Alex said. "And they're very scrappy — put up a real good fight. So we might catch a lingcod — they taste the best — or a greenling. They're not so big."

"Is it different from catching salmon? What do I do?"

"Light the buzz bombs," said Robyn. "Did you bring matches?"

Alex shook his head and laughed. "Don't listen to her, Sam. I'll show you, once we get started."

The boat cleared the spit and headed into the strait, then veered off toward the large island Sam recognized from the previous outing. "We're going to the same place! Trolling, right?" She gave Alex a triumphant smile as he lowered the throttle.

"Wrong, actually." After guiding the boat to a sheltered spot close to the island's rocky shore, he cut the engine. "This time we come to a complete halt."

"But all this — " Sam gestured to the thick tangle of brown seaweed. Big round bulbs like onions floated on the surface, their long blades streaming underneath. Snake-like stems coiled around the boat. What was it called? "Kelp!" she remembered. "Won't we get stuck?"

"Not a chance. Move over a bit so I can tie it up." He clambered to the bow and tied the boat to a sturdy kelp head. "This is what you call a makeshift anchor. The stem's attached to rocks down below, where the fish hang out. See that clear spot? Where there's an opening in the kelp bed? That's where you put your line." He returned to his seat and opened the tackle box. "What do you think, Robyn? Buzz bombs or jelly worms?"

"Jelly worms. Hand me a jig head and I'll set it up."

Buzz bombs, jig heads ... Sam never realized fishing had such a strange vocabulary. She looked on, fascinated, while Robyn took the jig head, a small chunk of lead attached to a sharp, curved hook. She picked out a rubbery beige worm and deftly threaded it on the hook, leaving the long tail end to curl behind. Waving it in front of Sam she said, "See how the tail end flicks? That's what'll attract the fish." She attached the lure to the fishing line. "Want to try?"

Sam hesitated.

"Go ahead," said Alex. "We'll tell you what to do."

"Sure, OK. Why not?" Sam grinned. This time she wouldn't get flustered. This time she'd catch a fish without losing the rod. Fishing for salmon had been a dismal failure, but jigging for cod, rockfish, whatever, would be a terrific success. Following her cousins' instructions, she began to let out the line.

"As soon as the line goes slack, you know it's hit bottom," Robyn said. "OK, now reel it up a bit. Careful it doesn't snag on the kelp. We'd have to yank it free, or else cut the line."

Sam reeled the line, praying it wouldn't snag.

"That's far enough," Alex said. "Now you lift the rod a couple of feet, then let it drop so the lure flutters down. Get it? Lift up and flutter down. When it drops, that's when the fish go for it."

Lift up and flutter down. Sam repeated the words to herself as she raised and lowered the line. Every few moments she reeled it in and checked to make sure the lure was still attached. Lift up and flutter down, lift up and flutter down …

"Ho hum." Robyn yawned. "You must be a jinx, Sam-bone. We should've had a bite by now."

Lift up and —

"Wait!" Sam felt a tug. "I've got something!"

"Reel it in!" cried Alex. "But careful, you might have snagged on something."

"Don't let go!" Robyn shouted.

Sam kept reeling. "It's coming, it's coming — and it feels heavy! Those jelly worms really work!"

She was glancing up to grin at Robyn when both cousins burst out laughing. "That's heavy?" Robyn smirked. "Look at it! It's all of five inches!"

Sam spotted the little fish twisting beneath the surface. Oh, well. At least this one wouldn't streak away with the rod. As soon as she reeled it in, she would let it off the hook.

Suddenly a large dark shape appeared. Before Sam could say "buzz bomb" — WHOOMP! The shape clamped onto the smaller fish.

Robyn shrieked with excitement.

"Wow!" cried Alex. "Look at the size of that sucker!"

"What is it?" Sam struggled to hold onto the rod. This time there was a *very* heavy something on the line. Each turn of the reel brought it closer, until she could make out its greyish-brown body and big ugly head.

"You've snagged a lingcod, a four or five pounder!" Alex exclaimed. "You want me to take the rod?"

"No! I can do it!" It was a struggle, but each turn of the reel brought the fish closer. "I've almost got it!" she squealed. "Oh, gosh, I hope it doesn't let go."

"It might," Alex said. "But it's not likely. They're not very smart. Plus they're territorial. They'll bite at anything. Jeez, he's a big one. Mom's going to freak. Quick, Robyn, get the net!"

But the fish was already in the boat, his jaws still clamped around the line. "Talk about pugnacious. He's still hanging on!" Alex grabbed the club and bonked the cod on the head. Then he opened its mouth and pulled out the smaller fish. "Now we can use the little guy for bait."

Sam's face fell. "But he's still alive. Can't you let him go?"

"Oh, great," said Robyn. "You're not going to wimp out on us, are you?"

"No ... "

"Good. Because I am." She caught hold of the wriggling fish, removed the hook, and watched it swim away. "We'll see how smart he is. Chances are he'll fall for it again. Nothing like an appetizing jelly worm. Yummers! Now it's my turn." She picked up the rod, checked the lure, and slowly let out the line.

"Aren't we going back now?" Since they'd already caught supper, Sam couldn't see the point of staying out any longer. Especially when things were going so well. What was that saying? *Quit while you're ahead.* She was definitely in favour of that.

But Alex wasn't ready to quit. "Nah, this is a great

spot. We should catch our limit, easy. You're not bored, are you?"

Sam shook her head and settled in the bow while her cousins took turns jigging for cod. It wouldn't be much longer, would it?

EIGHT

Big Mistake

One hour passed. Three smaller cod — all caught by Alex — joined Sam's big one. Robyn grumbled about her rotten luck.

The spot Alex had chosen was becoming less sheltered as the wind picked up, and soon Sam found herself gripping the sides of the boat. Was it supposed to be this rough? They couldn't catch anything with the boat rocking like crazy, could they? She was about to ask, but her words came out as a groan.

Don't be seasick, she told herself. Carsick was bad enough. Don't you *dare* be seasick …

Just as Sam's stomach gave another lurch, Robyn got a fish on the line. "Yahoo!" she cried. "Finally! Can you see it? There — in that seaweed." Alex leaned over to watch the struggle, the wind gave a sudden gust, and Sam hollered, "We're going to tip over!"

The twins were unconcerned. "Looks like another lingcod, even bigger than Sam's!" Alex exclaimed. "Way to go, Robyn!"

"Sam, grab the net, grab the net!" Robyn yelled. "This one's a fighter!"

Sam reached for the net and was handing it to Alex when the wind slammed a wave across the bow. Frightened, she dropped the net and clung to the boat. At the same instant, the fish gave a powerful tug and got away.

"Oh, no!" Robyn flung down the rod and glared at Sam. "Not again! All you had to do was hand me the net! Was that so big a problem?" She turned away in disgust.

Sam shrank into the bow, shaking not only from the queasiness in her stomach but from the unfairness of it all. It wasn't her fault. Robyn could have dropped the fish right into the boat. Alex could have grabbed the net. But she said nothing. Instead, she stared at the cod she'd reeled in earlier and thought how stupid it was to get itself caught. If it had just opened its big ugly mouth instead of trying to wolf down the little guy, it could have swum away, home free. After all, it hadn't been hooked.

By now the boat was rocking too much even for Alex to ignore. "Hey, Sam? Can you let go long enough to untie the rope?"

Her fingers felt numb from gripping the sides of the boat but she managed to untie the knot. Alex pulled the starter cord and in moments they were off.

As soon as they reached the other side of the island Sam realized how sheltered they had been. Wham! Waves smacked against the boat. The choppy sea foamed with whitecaps. If she'd felt sick with the rocking before, it was nothing compared to what they were facing now.

"Yee-haa!" Robyn exclaimed. "This is what I call bucking the waves!" Alex laughed along with his sister.

Sam held on so tightly her fingers turned blue. Every time they hit a wave the bow thumped down. Whack, whack ... She bit her lip, terrified the boat would dive into a trough and plunge straight down to the bottom of the sea. Or a giant wave would swamp them. Or she'd keel over the side. At least she was wearing a life jacket. But how long would she last in this freezing water? Whack! Her stomach reeled. Any minute now she'd lose breakfast and last night's supper combined. "Slow down, slow down!" she cried. If the twins heard her, they gave no sign.

Maybe if she sat on the floorboards it wouldn't be so bad? Maybe if she weren't perched up in the bow she wouldn't feel the waves so much? Maybe. But to get to the floor she had to move. And moving meant — Well, she couldn't. To release her grip was unthinkable. She was frozen, plain and simple. Once again she pleaded, "Slow down!" But the twins were having a terrific time. Obviously, bucking the waves was a favourite pastime.

Salt water streamed down her face. Her chest heaved, her stomach felt as if she'd swallowed two tons of brown kelp, and the eyes of the cod staring up at her didn't help matters one bit. As soon as they got back — *if* they got back — she'd tell Auntie Jean. She'd tell how her cousins had deliberately terrified her, just because she'd shown them up with her unexpected catch and then let Robyn's fish get away. She'd tell how much she hated them and how she wanted to go home.

"Isn't this great?" Alex's grin cracked his face from ear to ear.

Robyn faced Sam with a matching grin. "Better than a ride at the fair. Eh, Sam?"

Sam bit her lip so hard she tasted blood.

"Relax, Sam!" Alex shouted. "It's just a breeze, not a gale force wind. There's nothing to be scared about."

Who was he kidding? The amazing thing was, there were other boats on the strait. People smiled and waved as they zoomed past. Wasn't anybody worried? Didn't anybody care they were in the middle of a hurricane?

Each *thwump* of the bow brought them closer to the spit. Once around the point, the water was

calmer. Sam started to breathe again. Slowly she flexed her feet, legs, arms, fingers, surprised she could move them at all.

The dock was in sight. Closer, closer …

Finally. Without waiting for Alex to tie up the boat, Sam jumped out and ran toward the house.

"How did it go?" Auntie Jean greeted her cheerfully from the deck. "Are you ready for lunch?"

Sam rushed inside, ignoring her. She didn't want lunch. She didn't want cheerful. She wanted to tell, but of course she couldn't. It would only make matters worse.

Once in her room, she opened the top drawer of the dresser and pulled out her journal, remembering how excited she'd been at the prospect of filling up the pages. She had believed that everything she wrote would be wonderful.

Now, on the third day, she opened the journal to the first page and forced herself to write: *I made a mistake.*

For the millionth time she reminded herself it had been *her* idea to accept her aunt's invitation. "Please, Mom!" she had begged. "Auntie Jean's going to be in Toronto for that teachers' conference and she said I can fly back with her. It's not like I'm going by myself."

"Are you sure?" Mom said. "You're only ten, and it's so far."

"But by then I'll be eleven. The trip can be my birthday present."

"You've never been away before," said Dad. "And if — "

"I have so," Sam interrupted. "Last year at Brownie Camp, remember?"

"That wasn't on the other side of the country. And it was only five nights."

"Your cousins are a lot older than you," Mom said. "Wouldn't you rather go to camp again, with Angie?"

"No!" Camp was boring. The only time she'd enjoyed herself was when she'd led the raiding party to the fridge after lights out.

"Four weeks is a long time," Dad said. "You can't come tearing home if something goes wrong. Once you're there, you're there."

"*Puh-leeze!* It'll be an adventure! I've never been on a plane. I've never seen the ocean. I'm not a little kid anymore. And there's nothing to do here. Angie's away most of the time and you're working and Rupert's a boring old cat and I've read every book in the library already and you always say I should experience new things and take opportunities — "

"All right!" Dad held up his hands and gave Sam an I-give-up look. "If you're sure."

"Are you, Sam?" Mom still looked worried. "You

can't depend on Auntie Jean to amuse you. Uncle Lon will be away working most of the time, and your cousins are teenagers. They have interests that might not include a ten — sorry — eleven-year-old girl. You could be left to your own devices."

"I'm good at devices," Sam had said. "Anyway, Robyn and Alex want me to come. Auntie Jean says so in the letter."

"Well … "

"You'll see, Mom. It'll be wonderful."

Sam blinked back the tears and reread the words — *I made a mistake.* Then, having taken the plunge, she wrote on.

I thought the worst was over. After Robyn's fishing rod went overboard, thanks to me. But no.

This morning I went fishing with Robyn and Alex. Jigging for cod, they call it. I call it horrible. And I call them horrible. Alex and Robyn, I mean. Not the cod.

She went on to describe the morning, from sitting in the wrong seat when they first started off, to jumping out and running to her room, bleeding lip and all.

*At least I caught a fish and it didn't get
away. But I didn't really catch it. What a
stupid fish, to let itself get caught. And I'm
just as stupid because nobody hooked me
into coming here. I could have opened my
mouth and let go of the idea any time. And
stayed home.*

*Mom was right. My cousins, the Horribles,
don't want me here. I hate them and I'm
never going in their runabout again.*

She paused for a moment, tilted her pen, and
watched the elevator slide up and down the CN
tower. Then she took a sheet of notepaper and wrote
her first letter home.

Dear Mom and Dad,

*I am fine. Auntie Jean and Uncle Lon are
fine. Alex and Robyn are fine. Brackenwood
Point is fine, too. I've heard the foghorn and
last night I heard an owl. I have my own
room with no more ants and there's an
outhouse but we don't have to use it.*

*The day before yesterday we went fishing for
salmon. This morning we went jigging for
cod and I caught one. Auntie Jean is going to
cook it with a fancy sauce. I like fish and
chips better.*

Love, Sam

NINE

Left to Your Own Devices

After Sam failed the jigging-for-cod-and-bucking-the-waves test, the Horribles left her alone. Nothing was said, but it was understood. So when Auntie Jean asked why she wasn't going out with her cousins, Sam only said she'd rather explore the woods. Or collect seashells. Or read. Or write.

Every few days Auntie Jean drove to the village to do shopping or banking or whatever she had to do. Robyn and Alex usually went along, to visit friends or swim in the river. Sam stayed behind.

When it was too hot to do anything else, she splashed around in the ocean. The water was freezing, but after the first shock, she got used to it.

Uncle Lon told her the red rowboat was hers, if she wanted it. As long as she stayed near the point, within sight of the house. When the water was calm she put on her life jacket and rowed, remembering her lessons from Brownie Camp. Sometimes a seal popped up to keep her company.

She discovered a whole section of wildlife books in the living room, and studied pages of plants and animals that lived on the West Coast, in the woods or in the sea.

By the end of the first week, she knew the sounds of Brackenwood Point. And the names for practically everything. At dinner, when Uncle Lon quizzed her about her day, and Alex and Robyn teased her about the test, she was ready. Ebb and flow, sockeye, chinook, sea urchins, sculpins ... She knew them all.

Her favourite place in the woods was the old stump. One afternoon, she was sitting against it when she heard a rustling that wasn't the wind. Looking up from her book, she saw a movement in the ferns. A small brown face appeared, marked by a streak of white down the muzzle. Then a honey-coloured face, with white tips on the ears. Fawns!

They stepped out of the ferns on spindly legs, looking around with dark, curious eyes. A pattern of white spots covered their fur, blending in with the dappled light of the woods. No wonder Sam couldn't see them at first. Could they see her? Or did she blend in, too?

When the mother appeared, the fawns began to suckle. Sam grinned with delight.

Every afternoon she came to the woods and watched them nibbling on grasses and leaves. At first she was afraid to breathe in case she startled them. But after several days she could stand up quietly, pick huckleberries, and nibble right along with them.

One morning, Auntie Jean beckoned her onto the deck with a finger pressed to her lips. "Look!" she whispered, and pointed to the fawns.

Sam whispered back, "I've been watching them all week. But how come they're on their own? Has their mother left them? I can take care of them, can't I?" Wouldn't that be something to tell Angie, that she'd had two pet fawns.

"Oh, no, dear," her aunt said. "They're not abandoned."

"But something must have happened. The mother wouldn't just leave them."

"Deer leave their fawns to protect them. They don't have any scent for the first few weeks, so they can't attract predators. Unlike the mother."

"You mean the fawns are safer *without* their mother?"

Auntie Jean nodded. "Strange as it seems. But they always meet when it's time for a feed. See? Here comes Mom now."

They watched the fawns nuzzle up to their mother. "Aren't they lovely?" Auntie Jean said. "They can grow up and have all the nasturtiums they want."

Next to the stump in the woods, Sam's favourite place was the rocky promontory that jutted into the bay below the house. It was shaped like a ship, with a small depression where Sam could sit like a figurehead and gaze across the spit to the strait. Sometimes the seal appeared. She could see it swimming underwater, sleek as a torpedo.

At low tide she could walk for miles, listening to the slurps and gurgles and hisses of the beach, dodging the squirts of clams, and exploring tidepools. Sculpins darted out of hiding if she stirred the water. Hermit crabs scurried. Along the shoreline she found shells cast off by crabs. In the book Auntie Jean had given her, she'd learned that red rock crabs shed their outer skeleton when they grow, then find a protected place to wait for their new selves to harden. Like me, Sam thought. Her rock and her stump were safe places where her new self could harden. A self that could cope with the Horribles.

Her favourite tidepool residents were the ones with the impossible name that was sure to be on the test. *Anemone*. Not *anenome*. Either way they were beautiful creatures, more like flowers than animals. "They've got a strong sense of family," Uncle Lon had explained. "See how they're in clusters? With space in between? They won't mix beyond their own group. They sting another family if it gets too close."

Sam liked getting close. She would place her finger in the centre of an anemone and wait for the tickly feel as the feathery tentacles closed around it.

Barnacles of all shapes and sizes clung to the rocks. "They're stuck like glue," Auntie Jean said. "You try and pull one off."

Sam tried, unsuccessfully. What she liked about the barnacles was the way they got their food. As soon as the tide came up, out went their feet — tiny plumes that kicked food into their mouths. Uncle Lon had said, "Talk about playing with your food."

Sam would not have believed it, if it wasn't for the book. It sounded too much like something the Horribles would invent.

TEN

A Welcome Surprise

Early one morning, Sam sat on her rock watching wisps of fog swirl around the cove. The tide was way out. She counted eight herons, standing in the water. Why were they called great blue herons? They looked more grey than blue. They looked like layers of fog, standing still and silent, long necks bent as they waited to spear a fish. Without moving, they appeared and disappeared in the fog.

The scene reminded her of a poem she loved.

The fog comes in on little cat feet … She still knew it by heart, and remembered how astonished she'd been when her grade two teacher had printed it on the board, read it out loud, and said, "This is a poem." And it didn't even rhyme.

Here, she thought, the fog doesn't come in on little cat feet. It comes in like a heron. Tiptoeing stealthily, in slow motion. Long leg up, long leg down. Silent, silent as fog.

"Have a good time, honey," Mom had said. "Careful you don't lean against the fog."

Sam remembered how she had laughed. Mom always said that on the West Coast, the fog was so thick you could lean against it. But of course you couldn't.

What was fog, anyway? Only water, in a different form. In certain conditions, things change, she realized. At Brackenwood Point, conditions were different from home. So *she* was different. Even though she was still Sam, she felt unfamiliar to herself. It scared her, as if a part of her was still in Toronto. And until she got that part to join her, she'd be lost. She felt like a hermit crab, searching for a new shell to move into. Until it found one, it was lost. Vulnerable, Uncle Lon had said. Open to attack.

Attack from the Horribles. If she was like a crab, waiting for a shell, her cousins — especially Robyn — were anemones, stinging when anyone got too close to their territory.

Why hadn't things turned out the way she'd expected? *Don't lean against the fog.* Mom was right. Sam did have a way of counting on things too much. Imagining how perfect and wonderful something would be, then being disappointed when it didn't live up to expectations. But if you couldn't hope for the best, what point was there in hoping at all?

The sound of footsteps on the beach interrupted her thoughts.

"At least we don't have to take Gullible," Robyn was saying.

Sam crouched lower, hoping the edge of the rock would keep her hidden.

"Where is she?" Alex said.

"Who cares?"

"Come on, she's not so bad. For a city kid. And she's only eleven."

"Not so bad?" Sam could picture Robyn's lip curling into a sneer. "She's a disaster. She lost my rod and almost lost the net. She's a total wimp. And boring. All she does is wander around in the woods or sit on the beach. And when she rows, where does she go? Around the bay, in circles. And nobody could be that stupid, believing every little thing. What planet does she come from, anyway?"

"*Trawna,* remember?"

Robyn laughed and said something, but the sound of the boat being dragged across the gravel made it impossible to hear.

Trawna. What did they know about Toronto? Sam thought angrily. She'd like to see how well they made out in a big city. They'd feel as lost in her territory as she did in theirs.

She felt a prickling behind her eyes and struggled to hold back the tears. What she needed to do was something different. Something that would show the Horribles she wasn't a wimp. She'd wanted an adventure. Why not have one on her own? "I will, too! So there!" she shouted as the runabout sped away.

She jumped up from the rock, excited by the possibilities. She'd wait until after lunch, after the fog had lifted, but before it got windy. No one would know. The Horribles had taken the boat to Fisherman's Wharf to meet some friends. They'd be gone for hours. Uncle Lon wouldn't be home till late in the afternoon. That left Auntie Jean, but she always curled up with a book after lunch and would figure Sam was doing the same, either in the woods or on the beach. Not this time! She wouldn't tell her where she was going. That way everyone would be surprised when she came back, full of adventurous stories. And if nothing adventurous happened, she'd invent something.

She was so busy making plans she slipped into a tidepool and got a sneaker full of water. "Drat!" she exclaimed loudly, followed by, "Who cares?"

Inside, she sang as she rummaged for a new pair of socks. *Row, row, row your boat* ... Only this time, I'll go farther. This time I'll row around Brackenwood Point and explore the basin, all by myself. Then I'll show the Horribles — "

She stopped abruptly, feeling something hard in

the toe of her right foot. She pulled off the sock, gave it a shake, and laughed out loud as a dollar coin fell out. "Angie, you — !"

Angie had first lent her the loonie so she could buy a hot dog at the school Fun Fair. But when Sam went to pay her back, Angie said, "Forget it. I'm in a generous mood." A few days later Sam snuck into Angie's lunch kit at recess, carefully unwrapped a sandwich, and inserted the loonie between the lettuce and pepperoni. Angie never said a word. One month later, when Sam had completely forgotten about the loonie, she found it under her pillow. For over two years they had surprised each other, never knowing where or when the loonie would turn up. And now, here it was.

"Perfect timing, Angie!" Sam placed the coin on her thumb and flipped it, watching it spiral high in the air. It landed in her hand with a satisfying smack.

ELEVEN

Sam Courageous

The water was still, with the glassy-green tinge of Japanese fishing floats. As Sam rowed into the basin she noticed how the sea had nibbled the land, leaving sheltered bays and tucked-away coves. One cove was so hidden she didn't even see it until she reached the entrance. Then she saw the beach.

A maple tree grew on the bank. Some of its green leaves were already splashed with pale orange and gold. In the sunlight, the whole beach glowed.

Sam felt an irresistible pull. "It's like I'm the first person ever to be here!" she exclaimed. Drawing in the oars, she let the rowboat drift to shore.

In her mind, an adventure began to unfold. She saw herself as the captain of a ship, sailing into the basin for the first time. "Shall we go ashore?" she asked her imaginary crew.

"Oh no, Captain. We've heard ghostly rumours about this cove. It's not for the faint-of-heart."

"You cowards! Is there no one among you who will follow your captain, Sam Courageous? All right, then. I'll go alone."

When the boat reached shore, she jumped out and looped the rope around a rock. She waved to the ship anchored in the basin and bowed to the crew cheering on the decks.

Before she started exploring, she had to make her presence known. Real explorers always left a flag, but what could she use? Maybe some shedding arbutus bark? Yes, and a couple of maple leaves. She found a long pointed stick, stuck on two yellow leaves and a strip of the curling, reddish-brown arbutus bark, and planted the flag in the centre of the beach. Then she picked up a broken clamshell and carved *Sam* on a branch of the arbutus, followed by the date.

Before she set off for the woods, she found another stick, a stout one this time, in case of attack. "You never know what's out there," Alex had said when she'd wanted to explore Brackenwood on her own. "Watch out for the killer squirrels. And the mink with the razor blade teeth."

"Don't forget cougars," Robyn had added. "You'd be supper in no time. How brave are you, anyway?"

"We'll see who's brave," Sam muttered. "We'll see who's just a city kid. And we'll see who's *not* falling for your dumb stories anymore."

A squirrel peered down from a hemlock branch and chittered in alarm as she fought through the brush. Deeper in the woods, skyscrapers of cedar and fir blocked the sun. A rocky outcrop looked promising. If she climbed to the top, she might have a view of the basin. Then she could see how far she'd gone. She clambered up the moss-covered rock, using the tough sword ferns as a climbing rope, and crevices in the rock for toeholds.

When she reached the top, a meadow stretched before her, its tall grass bleached to a tawny gold. She could no more see the sea from here than she could from down below. But it was sunny and warm, a good spot for a rest. She leaned against a mossy log, hidden by tall clusters of ferns. Sitting as still as a heron, she watched two dragonflies circle the meadow. Pine white butterflies fluttered by without a sound …

Sam opened her eyes with a start. How long have I been sitting here? she wondered. The meadow was still in sunlight but the shadows appeared longer. And the wind had definitely picked up.

Uh, oh. If it was windy in this sheltered meadow, how windy would it be on the basin? How would she manage to row back?

Putting it off would not make it easier. And you're Sam Courageous, her inner voice prodded. You're setting an example for your crew, right?

Right!

She was about to get up when she noticed something moving. Something that blended in so completely with the dried grass she could almost convince herself it wasn't there. Was it a fawn?

No …

This something was bigger than a fawn.

She spotted two black ears appearing above the grass, followed by a small head. Yellow eyes, long whiskers —

A cat. A very large cat.

She froze as the animal stirred to its feet.

It wasn't a cat.

At least, not an ordinary cat.

TWELVE

More Surprises

No question about it. Sam had read enough of her aunt's wildlife books to know that the animal at the far edge of the meadow was a cougar.

His thick coat was tawny on the sides, shoulders and haunches. The long fur on his throat and belly was lighter, mottled with white, sandy-grey, and tan. Along the ridge of his back was a reddish-brown streak, darkening to black at the tip of his round, heavy tail. Compared to the rest of his low-slung body, his head was small, with patches of white fur above the eyes. A black patch below the nose looked like a butterfly resting on his upper lip.

As Sam watched, the cougar yawned, flexed his muscles, dug his claws into the ground, and stretched. Then he sat on his haunches, and with a twitch of his tail, daintily began licking a paw. He looked so much like Rupert she almost laughed out loud. Until it hit her.

This wasn't a pet cat. This was a wild cougar. And in spite of the mild, pleasant look on his face, Sam knew she had reason to be afraid. So far, the cougar hadn't seen her. But what if he picked up her scent? She gripped the stick lying across her knees and prayed that he would go away — in the opposite direction — so she could run to safety.

Just when she thought he was leaving, she heard a rasping whistle farther off in the grass. The cougar stopped and turned, then answered with a chirping meow. And as the grass stirred again, Sam discovered the cougar wasn't a him, but a her.

A kitten stumbled across the grass, followed by another. Both had pale tawny coats, dappled with penny-sized patches of rusty-brown fur. Streaks of the same dark colour ringed their tails and stubby bow legs. One, Sam noticed, had a dark brown stripe running the length of its tail. The other had a black mustache mark on either side of its nose.

Instead of leading her kittens away, the mother stretched out in the meadow and dozed, purring contentedly. Sam watched the kittens climb all over the big cat, nuzzling her ears and swatting the tip of her tail as it flicked lazily back and forth. When they tired of that game, they pounced on leaves whirling down from the alders, and leaped at butterflies, trying to catch them. Sam became so wrapped up in their antics she forgot to feel afraid, and began to breathe more easily. She even caught herself smiling.

The kittens wrestled and rolled and tumbled in the grass, stumbling over clumsy paws that seemed too big for the rest of them. For awhile they played at stalking each other. Then, as if that game made them hungry, they curled up against their mother for a snack. They suckled greedily, until she decided it was time to leave. She got up, nosed the kittens, and padded silently toward the woods. With every step, the muscles rippled in her legs and shoulders. She paused frequently, to sniff the air. Her kittens frisked ahead.

Sam followed them with her eyes until they were well out of sight. Even then, she remained still, memorizing every detail from the sound of the wind to the smell of the sea. Finally she got up, stretched her cramped muscles, and raced back to the beach.

"COUGAR!" she shouted. "I've seen a real, live cougar! *This* close!" She threw her arms around the smooth trunk of the arbutus and gave it a fierce hug. "A cougar! And her *kittens!*"

And because the whole wonderful, magical, terrifying, awesome experience needed something more, she carved *COUGAR* in huge letters below her name.

She couldn't wait to get back and tell everyone. Talk about adventure! Robyn would never again call her a wimp. Never, never —

Suddenly, she stopped. Something was missing. And with a growing sense of horror, she realized what it was.

The rowboat was gone.

THIRTEEN

Another Mistake

"It can't be!" Sam cried. The rowboat couldn't have drifted away. She'd tied it up, hadn't she? She *couldn't* have just looped the rope around a rock and left it. Maybe she had come back to the wrong place. She was about to scramble over the rocks and check the next beach when she realized that of course this was the beach — hadn't she carved her name to prove it? And that stick with the wilted leaves and drooping bark — wasn't that her flag? So what happened?

Obviously the tide had gone out and taken the rowboat with it. Obviously the great Sam Courageous had not tied it up properly. Some captain she turned out to be.

She squinted her eyes and looked out at the basin. Was that a speck of red?

Yes. That was the rowboat all right, drifting farther and farther away.

For a moment, she caught herself wishing the Horribles were around. They'd know what to do. But then, they would have made sure the boat was securely fastened in the first placé.

She could yell to attract attention, but there was no one in sight. Even the sailboat she'd seen earlier was gone. Well then, the only thing to do was hike through the woods until she found the road.

Oh, sure, said her inner voice. There's a cougar in the woods, remember? A fiercely protective *mother* cougar.

Her heart skipped a beat. But I read that they're shy, she argued. They don't like being near humans. So if I make a lot of noise the cougar will know I'm coming and stay away. She's probably on the other side of her territory by now. Or back in the den with her kittens.

Or looking for supper, said the voice. They *do* sometimes attack humans. Especially little kids who look like prey.

OK. I'll stay out of the woods.

Then how will you get back?

Finally, after seesawing back and forth, she gave up arguing and decided to go for the woods. The road couldn't be that far.

She picked up her stick and a large rock, and making as much noise as possible, retraced her steps to the meadow. Now what? She glanced around nervously. Which way should I go?

She remembered that Brackenwood Point faced the setting sun. How could she forget? Every night Uncle Lon was on the deck with his camera, oohing and ahhing over the sunset. It wasn't sunset time yet, but if she followed the sun, she'd be going in the right direction. Or close enough.

Pleased with her reasoning, she left the meadow, walking through shady woods toward the sun. She banged her stick against the rock, loudly singing, "Jingle Bells." Hardly the season for it, she admitted, but the first song that came into her mind.

She struggled through ocean spray, snowberry bushes and tangles of scratchy Oregon grape, only to find herself faced with an impassable thicket of prickly salmonberry. There was nothing to do but go around it, but first she stopped to eat a few juicy yellow-orange berries.

She set off again, careful to avoid a dense patch of dark green stinging nettle. One brief encounter with that plant was enough. Alex had warned her, but not before the stinging hairs covering the leaves had touched her hands. The tingling had lasted a whole afternoon, and no amount of rubbing with soap — which Robyn swore was the only cure — had relieved the burning pain. And to think Auntie Jean picked the new shoots every spring and steamed them. Then *ate* them! Like spinach! Yuck!

Avoiding the stinging nettle took her away from the path of the sun and straight to a pond. She made her way around the edge, stumbling through cat-tails and clumps of bright green skunk cabbage. She was battling a thick patch of salal when a thought struck her. *She should have stayed on the beach.* Then, when she wasn't back for supper, Auntie Jean would worry and Uncle Lon would go out in the cabin cruiser to look for her. She would shout and wave her flag and be rescued. Why hadn't she thought of that sooner? There was only one thing to do. Go back around the pond and return to the beach.

This time, she sang "The Ants Came Marching One by One." On each "Hurrah!" she gave the trees a vigorous whack. By the time the ants came marching "twenty by twenty" she was tired of thinking up rhymes for what the little ant did whenever he stopped. And she still hadn't reached the spot where she'd first come upon the pond. There had to be a shortcut.

She stopped to get her bearings. "OK … The stinging nettles are over there, so I came from that direction. And the meadow was way back behind those trees — so if I go up over this rock, I'll get to the meadow much faster, and from there it's a piece of cake."

For a change of pace she sang her old kindergarten favourite, "The Cat Came Back," hoping that the cougar cat wouldn't. By the fourth time through she had reached the top of the rock. And realized it hadn't led her to the meadow, but deeper into the woods.

As she looked around, the full weight of it hit her.

In a trembling voice she said, "I'm lost."

FOURTEEN

Lost

What to do?

Don't panic. And stay put.

This time there was no arguing with the voice. She remembered being lost in Toronto's Eaton Centre one Christmas. When Mom finally found her, she had made Sam promise that *next* time she got lost, she was not to budge. She had to plant herself in one place and stay there.

But how long will I have to stay here? she wondered. And where *was* here?

Everything had changed. She had been so intent on getting back to the beach, she hadn't noticed the fog creeping in. Now, nothing seemed real. The trees looked like shadows painted on a white backdrop, a backdrop that pressed in on all sides.

Uncle Lon would come looking for her, that was certain. And eventually he would find her. It wasn't like she was in the middle of the Rocky Mountains. But what if she'd wandered into the wilderness park? How big did Alex say it was? Over three thousand acres.

She passed a hand in front of her face, as if clearing it of cobwebs. The fog muddled everything. Where was West, now? Where was anything?

Her lower lip trembled. This whole trip she'd been leaning against the fog, expecting everything to be wonderful. Now here she was, lost in the fog. What if she wasn't found before nightfall? The thought made her shudder.

What would the Horribles do? And what would Angie do?

Build a shelter. At least that would give her something to do. It would keep her warm, too, in case she had to stay out all night.

All night? She pushed down the rising sense of panic. I won't think about night, she told herself. But I will do something to stay warm.

She tore branches off a hemlock tree, then gathered them up and piled them against a log, making a soft mattress. On top she spread layers of the draping grey-green lichen Robyn called "witch's hair." When her "bed" was ready, she lay down, ignoring the scratchy feel of lichen on her bare arms and legs. Next time, she caught herself thinking, I'll bring jeans and a jacket, maybe even —

What do you mean, *next* time? her inner voice scolded. You won't get lost, next time.

She covered her body with extra branches and ferns, from the tips of her toes to the top of her head. That done, she lay snug under her hemlock quilt. She welcomed the familiar sounds: the muffled thumps of fir cones dropping to the ground, the nagging of a Stellar Jay, the drumming of a red-headed flicker boring into a trunk for insects, the grating *crruuk* of a raven flying from a cedar branch. In the distance, she heard the foghorn and found it comforting.

The growling of her stomach was less comforting. If I ever go anywhere again, she vowed, I'll be prepared. I'll fill my backpack with everything, just in case. Especially food. She should've eaten more salmonberries. And hadn't she passed a huckleberry tree? Somewhere by the pond? Should she go and look?

No. Stay put.

Scratches from tramping through the bushes criss-crossed her arms and legs, and she had mosquito bites on her neck and behind her knees. She gave them an absent-minded scratch. At least she hadn't stepped in a wasp's nest.

On the last day of Brownie Camp she and Angie had walked around the lake during Free Time, joking about how much fun it would be to get lost. Together, of course. It was a safe joke, since they were always within sight of the lodge and never wandered off the path. Except once, when Angie had to go to the bathroom. Heading for the bushes, they walked straight into a wasp's nest.

"YEOWW!" They jumped back, screaming, waving their arms and stamping their feet. Instead of driving off the wasps, it made them madder.

"I'm allergic!" Angie howled. "I'm going to DIE!"

"Me too!" Sam cried all the way back to the lodge. How could anything hurt so much? She counted six stings on her legs and arms, every one an explosion of pain that stabbed like a red-hot needle.

Angie had one sting, on her thumb. But that one sting made her arm swell up ten times its normal size.

"Too bad it wasn't your toe," Sam said when Angie came back from the doctor's. "You'd be a Bigfoot."

"You can laugh," Angie had said.

Sam had read somewhere that if you step into a wasp's nest and stand absolutely still they don't hurt you. They just think you're a stump or something, and buzz off. Would she be brave enough to do that? Stand among wasps without moving?

Somehow, she didn't think so.

Anyway, that wouldn't be brave. That would be stupid. There was a difference. Brave was sitting very still and watching a cougar. Stupid was not tying up the rowboat.

To take her mind off the boat and to keep the cougar away — just in case — she sang a few more verses of "The Cat Came Back." But singing didn't keep the worries away.

What happens when it gets dark? she thought fearfully. I can't keep singing all night. And what if the cougar comes? What if the cougar's stalking something in the woods and accidentally finds me? Maybe right now, this very second, the cougar's stalking through the fog, getting closer and closer and closer …

Her heart beat faster. What was that rustling sound? Was something moving through the bushes?

"Ohh!" Something between a squeak and a moan escaped her lips, and she clamped her mouth shut to keep from crying out loud. Her heart stopped beating altogether. Here it comes! she panicked. A sudden pounce and the cougar —

Don't be stupid! It couldn't be a cougar. Cougars move silently.

Whew! She breathed more easily. The rustling was probably a deer. That would be wonderful, to have a deer nearby to keep her company. Better yet, one of the fawns!

Wait a minute. Now something was *crashing* through the bushes. Too big for a fawn. Too loud for a deer. Her heart dropped to the pit of her stomach. What if it was a bear? She'd forgotten about bears. What if —

"SAM? ARE YOU THERE?"

"SAMANNNTHA!"

Voices echoed through the fog.

"OVER HERE!" she hollered, pushing the hemlock branches aside. She jumped up and down, resisting the urge to run toward the voices in case she got lost again. "HERE, HERE!"

Suddenly Uncle Lon burst through the bushes, followed by another man. Sam ran into her uncle's outstretched arms and gave him a ferocious hug. "I'm so glad to see you!"

"That makes two of us. Boy, you had us worried." He blew two ear-splitting blasts on his whistle and waited until he heard a three-blast response. "That's Alex," he said. "He and Robyn started searching from the beach. Now they can head on home. This is our neighbour by the way, Mr. Duncan. Owns the sheep farm next door. We came in from the road."

"Is it far?"

"A couple of miles. Nothing a city slicker like you can't handle. Unless you'd like a piggyback?"

"Yes, please." Sam climbed onto his back gratefully. She'd had enough of being brave for one day.

"Sam, we've been worried sick. And I must say I'm a bit disappointed." Auntie Jean's tone was firm but not unkind. "What were you told when we said you could use the rowboat?"

Sam chewed her dinner roll, swallowed, then said quietly, "Stay near the point. Within sight of the house."

"That's right. From now on, no rowing off on your own. If you want to go for a row, you make sure Robyn or Alex is with you."

"But Mom," Robyn protested, "it wasn't the rowing that got her in trouble, it was — "

"Robyn," her father said sternly, "if your attitude doesn't change, you're away from boats for the rest of the summer. I hold you partly to blame for this. If you'd been more pleasant, Sam wouldn't have been so anxious to go off by herself. Am I right? Well?"

There was a long pause. Finally, Robyn lowered her eyes and said, "Yes."

For a few moments, no one spoke. Then Alex passed Sam another roll and said, "When we saw the rowboat in the middle of the basin we thought you'd fallen overboard and drowned. We were frantic. Especially when we saw your life jacket on the seat, and the oars pulled in. Then Mr. Duncan came sailing past and said he'd seen the rowboat on the beach hours ago but no one in sight. So we figured it out. What took you so long, anyway? Were the woods that interesting?"

Sam looked up from her third bowl of clam chowder and saw that everyone was watching her, waiting for an explanation. But what could she say? Her experience with the cougar was too special to be spoken of lightly. She wanted them to share not only her excitement, but also her sense of wonder. If she started at the beginning and set the scene, maybe she could draw them into the experience so they would understand.

But first she had to apologize. "I'm sorry," she said. "For getting you worried. I didn't mean to. I know I should've tied up the boat and not wandered off, but when I tell you — " She paused and took a breath. "When I tell you what happened — "

"So, tell!" Robyn said eagerly. "We're all waiting."

"OK." Sam smiled, remembering. "I was exploring the woods and wasn't exactly sure where I was, so I climbed up this rock — it was really steep — to see if I could see the basin. And at the top, I came to this meadow. It was sunny and warm and I sat down for a rest — "

"And you fell asleep?" Robyn interrupted. "We spent hours searching for you because you decided to take a nap?"

"No!" Sam gave her cousin an angry look. "It was only for a second, but when I woke up, a cougar was there!"

"A cougar?" Alex snorted with disbelief. "And I'm a blue beluga."

"It *was!* And she had two kittens, and I sat and watched them playing and as soon as they left — "

"Come on, Sam!" Robyn laughed. "Do you honestly think you could sit there without a cougar knowing?"

"I wasn't that close, and I was hidden in the ferns,

and I was really quiet."

"Are you sure those wildlife books aren't giving you ideas?" Uncle Lon said kindly.

"She's trying to turn us into Gullibles," said Robyn. "Nice try, Sam-bone."

"That's enough, Robyn." Auntie Jean turned to Sam. "You've had quite a day, haven't you, honey? It was smart of you to build a shelter. Lon told me you did a terrific job."

"Thanks." Sam gave her aunt a grateful smile. At least she'd done something right.

Before she went to sleep, Sam curled up on the bed with her journal and spilled her story of the cougar onto the clean page.

For a long time afterwards, she sat looking out the window, watching the night settle over the woods. Somewhere out there — somewhere — was a cougar with two kittens. And she was probably the only person in the world who had seen them.

The thought made her shivery, all over.

FIFTEEN

Summer Days

July sweltered to an end. The Horribles had been planning their fifteenth birthday party, but since Robyn's friend Kate wasn't back from holidays, they decided to postpone the party until Labour Day. Sam mentally thanked the unknown Kate for being away. The thought of Brackenwood being invaded by a bunch of her cousins' friends was enough to drive her into a kelp bed.

On July 30, the day before the twins' birthday,

Sam went to the village with Auntie Jean and bought Robyn a new fishing rod. "Guaranteed not to fall overboard," she said when Robyn opened the present.

Robyn chuckled. "Thanks, Sam. Maybe I'll catch my lost fishing rod with this one. Stranger things have happened."

She gave Alex a bag of jelly worms — the fruit-flavoured kind — with a few Gummi Bears thrown in. "Guaranteed *not* to catch cod," she said.

They celebrated the birthday with a wiener roast on the beach, a welcome change from the usual fare of clam chowder, crab, cod and salmon. When Sam asked why they always ate seafood, her uncle told her the whole family was on a seafood diet.

"Oh! That explains it," she said.

Then he added, "We see food and we eat it."

She was beginning to see where the twins got their teasing from.

For the first week of August, the days followed a pattern. Patches of early morning fog. Clear skies and high temperatures by noon, with winds gusting in the afternoon. Because of the wind, Sam avoided the runabout, even though the twins kept asking her to join them. And since she wasn't allowed to go rowing by herself, she spent the days on shore.

She collected shells, pressed ferns in her book, and sat against her stump, watching the fawns. Often, it wasn't the fawns she was seeing. It was the cougar kittens, jumping at butterflies, tripping over their big feet. And their mother, licking them as they nuzzled against her. Sam framed the pictures in her mind, as real as any photographs could be.

Even as she watched the herons tiptoe through the fog, her mind slipped back to the cougars. Out there, in the wilderness, somewhere. She hoped they were safe.

On a trip to the village, Auntie Jean took her to the library. Sam hunted through the animal section and took out every available book on cougars.

Evenings were cool with the fog rolling in. Uncle Lon always built a fire, and everyone read or watched TV or played cards. Sam devoured the cougar books for more information, then wrote what she discovered in her journal.

"A professor of cougarology," Uncle Lon said with a grin, watching her one evening. "That's what you are."

"Dreamology's more like it," said Robyn.

Sam ignored her and grinned back at her uncle. He probably didn't believe she'd seen a cougar any more than the others did, but she didn't care.

A change in the weather brought an end to the wind and welcome relief from the heat. Rain woke Sam, one night. As she listened to it drumming on the roof, she realized, with a sense of shock, she only had one week left.

SIXTEEN

Quimper Bay

"We're going to Quimper Bay," Robyn said next morning. "And this time Gullible's coming."

"As long as it doesn't get windy," Sam added.

"Not a chance," said Uncle Lon. "The rain's cleared the air. It's like a mirror out there. But don't stay out too long. And if you do any exploring, make sure you stick together."

"You want a lunch?" Auntie Jean asked. "There's a lovely beach."

"I'll make it," Sam volunteered. She bustled about while her cousins got the boat ready. In a few minutes they were ready to go.

"You don't have to sit on the floorboards," Alex said. "There's a seat, remember?"

"It's too tippy, sitting up there." In spite of her uncle's assurances, Sam hadn't forgotten the disastrous day of the whitecaps. Wind or no wind, she was staying on the floor.

Alex pulled the cord on the outboard. Soon they were speeding toward the strait.

"What's in here, anyway?" said Robyn, shifting Sam's backpack.

Sam had decided she wasn't going to make the same mistake twice. "A whistle in case we get lost. Matches and a flashlight in case it gets dark. And sandwiches and Kool-aid for lunch."

"What kind of sandwiches did you make?"

Sam smiled. "You'll see."

"Do you want to come to the creek with us?" Robyn asked when they reached Quimper Bay. "It's just over there."

"No thanks," said Sam. "I'll stay here." She watched the twins chase each other across the beach, then disappear in the bushes beside the creek. Whew!

Now she could explore the beach in peace.

She collected stones as white as peppermints and shells shaped like turbans. She placed them on a log, making starfish patterns. White stone, black stone, speckled stone, wishing stone. Clamshell, limpet shell, mussel shell —

"Bear tracks!" The cousins raced back, shrieking. "In the mud, beside the creek! *Huge* tracks! Gigantic!"

Before she knew it, Sam was in the boat, fastening her life jacket.

"Gotcha!" The twins laughed. When they caught their breath, Alex said, "Do you want to explore the woods with us? It's too hot sitting around here."

"Nope," said Sam. "I like it here."

Robyn shook her head in amazement. "You're brave enough to go traipsing through the woods by yourself but you're too scared to come with us?"

"I'm not scared. I just don't want to."

"You're not going to wander off and get lost again, are you?" Robyn said. "We're supposed to stay together."

"I won't leave the beach. I promise."

"OK," said Alex. "But you'll be sorry you missed these woods. If the Sasquatch comes, or the bear — the real one that is, not the one we made up — scream. We'll come running."

Sam waved them off and continued with her collection. She added odd-shaped pieces of green sea glass, and a lacy clump of dried seaweed. She spied on several purple and orange starfish clinging to the rocks, and teased the pink anemones in the tidepools. Then she leaned against a weathered log, picking up handfuls of pebbles and listening as they trickled through her fingers.

It wasn't long before she was wishing she had gone with her cousins. For the last week or so, they hadn't been so horrible. Robyn had even been nice, talking to her like a real person, and asking her about life in Toronto. Maybe the new fishing rod had something to do with the change. Maybe it was because Kate would soon be home. Or maybe she just got tired of being miserable.

The twins still teased her, to see if she'd take the bait — like the "strip teasers" Uncle Lon used for catching salmon. When she didn't bite, they left her alone. Lately, she'd been so preoccupied with her "cougarology" she hadn't paid much attention to them. And it didn't matter how much they teased her about seeing things. *She* knew what she'd seen.

Anyway, the twins' teasing didn't seem as mean as it had before. Or maybe her new self was hardening. She was beginning to feel more at home, like a hermit crab who'd finally found a new shell.

That thought convinced her. Quickly, she grabbed her backpack, scrambled up the bank, and found her cousins waiting at the top.

"We figured you'd come eventually," said Alex. "Being a curious and adventurous kind of person."

Sam gave him a pleased smile.

They walked without speaking, following the path

through the woods. Sam walked in the middle, enjoying the twins' silence as much as the sounds of the forest. The chitter of a squirrel, a brushing of needles, the flap of wings. She had the eerie feeling she was being watched, but whenever she turned around, there was nothing there.

Farther along, she glanced over her shoulder and saw a flash of tan in the underbrush. A dead leaf? Turning again, she caught another glimpse of tan, this time at the edge of the path.

There *was* something there.

Her cousins would have to believe her. Making her voice calm, she said, "Have you ever seen a cougar?"

Robyn groaned. "Not cougars, again. Honestly."

Sam pressed on. "What would *you* do if you saw a cougar? Not if you were watching from a distance, but if you saw one up close."

"Look tough, throw stuff and make a lot of noise," said Alex. "That's what you're supposed to do."

"Good thing I brought my pack."

"Why?"

"To throw at the cougar."

"What cougar?"

"The one following us."

"Nice try, Gullible." But they turned around anyway.

And stopped cold.

SEVENTEEN

Run!

Sam didn't stop to think. She hurled her backpack. Waved her arms. Jumped up and down to make herself big. And shouted and roared and screamed.

The startled cougar bounded into the underbrush. In two tremendous leaps it had climbed the rockface and disappeared over the top.

"RUN!" the twins yelled. "RUN!"

Sam grabbed her pack and raced along the trail. Out of the forest, down the bank, onto the beach

and into the boat.

"Did you see it? The way it stood there and stared?"

"That was a cougar! A real cougar!"

"You should have seen how *big* you looked," Robyn said. "And *loud!* They must've heard you in Victoria! No wonder you got to be the giant. Honestly, Sam. I couldn't swallow, let alone scream. I was so totally petrified."

"Hey, Sam — are you OK? Aren't you going to say something?"

Sam resisted the impulse to say, "I told you so." But her look was unmistakeable.

"You win," said Alex. "You really did see a cougar. We believe you."

"I wonder where the kittens are," Robyn said. "Mother cougars go crazy when they're protecting their young. We're so lucky we escaped."

Excitement made them hungry. As the boat drifted in the bay they opened Sam's pack and gobbled up the sandwiches. "Sure you don't want one?"

Sam shook her head. She thought for awhile, looking from one twin to the other. Then she said, "Does your tongue feel fuzzy yet? Is your mouth starting to itch?"

Alex and Robyn looked at each other. "No ... "

"You know that green stuff in your sandwich?"

"Yeah ... "

"Stinging nettle."

"AAGH!" They gagged and gulped down the rest

of the Kool-aid.

"Is it sweet enough? I put in lots of sugar — I think it was sugar — but I couldn't get the colour right. I used water from the creek. You know that little pool near the skunk cabbages?"

"AAUGH!" They sputtered and spat over the side. "Not *that* water! AAUGH!"

"Gotcha," Sam whispered under her breath. She grinned all the way home.

"You did exactly the right thing," Uncle Lon said later. "Act like you're a threat, not prey. And good thing you didn't run until after it was gone. A cougar will instinctively give chase, and there's no hope of out-running one. Good grief! Face to face with a cougar! Guess it's the same one you saw. Eh, Sam? Can't doubt your word now."

But something was bothering Sam. "I don't think it was," she said. "This one was darker and the other — "

"Yeah, right," Robyn interrupted. "Like there's two full-grown cougars in the same spot? I don't think so."

"I wouldn't be so sure," her mother said. "The one you saw today could be a young male looking for new territory. They do that, don't they, Sam?"

Sam nodded. "I read that once they're over a year

old, usually around eighteen months, they leave their mother and wander around till they find a place of their own. They travel a long ways, sometimes."

"This one could've come down from the hills, travelled to the end of the spit and swum across to the park. You kids stay close to home for awhile. No more exploring in the woods."

"Ahh, Mom!" Alex complained. "He's long gone, now. Sam scared him off."

His father frowned. "I wouldn't bet on that."

EIGHTEEN

Counting Sheep

Next morning, Sam was up with the herons. But even though she looked in their direction, she wasn't seeing them. Once again, her mind was in a sunlit meadow, watching two cougar kittens.

"Morning, Sam." She turned to see her uncle, accompanied by a tall, dark-haired man in a uniform. "This is Mr. Pendray, the conservation officer. Joel, my niece Samantha. We call her Sam."

Mr. Pendray smiled. "So you're the girl who saw

the cougar."

"Robyn and Alex did, too," Sam said. "It was in the park."

"It's the other one I'd like to hear about, first. The one with — "

" — the kittens?" Sam's smile grew as she described the scene.

"And you're sure the mother wasn't gold-coloured all over?"

"No way. Her ears were black, and she had a black butterfly shape around her muzzle and a black tip on her tail."

Mr. Pendray looked pleased. "I always ask that question when there's been a sighting. So many people swear they've seen a cougar, even in the city. But if they say there wasn't a speck of black I know they've been seeing one tabby too many."

A thought suddenly struck Sam. "You're not going to shoot her, are you?"

"Heck, no. She wasn't bothering anybody, was she? And she's in her own territory, after all. I'm curious about the other one, though. The big fellow you saw in the park. You're sure it wasn't the same one?"

"Positive! It was a lot darker, almost chestnut. And — "

"Joel!" Auntie Jean called out from the deck. "Matt Duncan's on the phone. You better come quick."

Sam gave her uncle a worried look. "Mr. Duncan has sheep, doesn't he?"

Her uncle nodded. "Could be he has one less."

Uncle Lon was right. A short time later, Joel Pendray returned from Mr. Duncan's farm with the news that one ewe had been killed. "A contract hunter's on his way with his two hounds," he said.

"Bloodhounds?" asked Alex.

"No, blueticks. They're smaller than bloodhounds, but darned good trackers. Nothing we can do till they get here."

"You've got time for coffee, then," Auntie Jean said. "Freshly brewed mocha java?"

"Twist my arm!" He joined them on the deck and took a sip of coffee. Then he continued with the matter at hand. "He's probably a young male cougar. That's the trouble, you see — these young fellas haven't established their own territory so they wander, a bit confused ... Heck, they don't know the difference between someone's pet dog or a sheep or a deer. It's all meat to them. And do they go through it! You know how much meat there is in thirty-six hamburgers? That's what a cougar needs every day. Now, a deer will last them a week or so — they can't eat the whole thing in one meal. And when it's gone, they'll kill another one. Mmm ... " He paused as Auntie Jean passed him a plate of carrot-pineapple muffins. "Don't mind if I do."

"You should shoot it, if it's killing sheep," said Robyn.

"Cougars are carnivores. They do what they have to do to get food."

"Well, still. It could've attacked us."

"There was certainly that possibility. You kids did the right thing. But you know, the odds of being attacked by a cougar are about the same as being struck by lightning. Heck, in the past hundred years, here in B.C. there's been fewer than ten deaths caused by cougars."

"Why was it following us?" Alex wondered. "Has that happened before?"

"Sure. Cougars often follow hikers, just out of curiosity."

"As for killing sheep," Uncle Lon said, "Matt Duncan will be the first to admit he's had more sheep killed by dogs than by cougars."

"How do you know this sheep was killed by a cougar?" Sam asked. "It could've been a dog, couldn't it?"

"Oh, it was a cougar, no doubt about that. For one thing, the sheep was killed quickly. You can tell by the puncture wounds in the skull. You don't get a clean kill like that with dogs." He paused while Uncle Lon poured him a second cup of coffee. "For another thing, after he killed the sheep, he dragged it into the underbrush. Ate up the organs and lungs—"

"*Gross!*" Robyn interjected.

" — then went off a short distance to sleep. That's what they do. All that eating, not to mention stalking, killing and dragging, usually tires them out. But he plans to come back."

"How do you know?"

"He left his 'I'm coming back' sign. Covered the carcass with dirt, leaves, twigs and grass, to hide it from ravens and eagles and turkey vultures. Later on, he'll come back and finish eating. Whenever we're looking for a cougar, we start from the kill, if we can. The cat will usually be close by. That's one thing in our favour — a cougar is easily treed on a full tummy. He's not in the mood for a long-distance run."

"Like us after Christmas dinner," Alex remarked. "Or if we ate thirty-six hamburgers."

"Exactly," said Mr. Pendray. "As soon as the hounds get here, we'll track the cat and — "

"Shoot him," said Robyn.

"No, no, only as a last resort. We'll anesthetize him, then relocate him far from here. If he's killed one sheep, he might kill more."

"Do you use a dart gun?" Alex asked.

"We use a single-barrelled shotgun made specially for darts. The tranquillizers get put in the dart tube, along with the needle. Trouble is, the drugs lose their potency if they're pre-mixed, so I have to wait till the animal is treed or cornered, then mix the drugs. Takes about five, ten minutes to set it all up. Gets a bit stressful, sometimes. Especially if you've got a TV camera looming over your shoulder. That often happens, especially if the cat's cornered somewhere in the city and the media gets wind of it. I remember this one time … "

His story was interrupted by the ringing of the phone, and the message that the hounds had arrived at the Duncan farm. "I'm on my way," he said, getting up to leave. "Thanks for the coffee and muffins, Jean. Say, Lon — Ever been on a cougar hunt?"

"No ... "

"It's safe enough, as long as you stay close to us. Want to come?"

"You mean it? I'd love to!"

Sam thought her uncle's face would split in half, he was so excited. As she watched them go, it occurred to her that if it was safe enough for Uncle Lon, it would be safe enough for anybody. Why not her? She could hike through the woods and keep up with the others, staying out of sight if necessary. And unlike the cougar, she didn't have a full stomach. She could do a long-distance run, easy.

"Earth to Sam!" Robyn waved a hand in front of her face. "Want to go out in the rowboat?"

"Or the runabout?" said Alex. "It's not windy."

"What? No, sorry. I'm going to write a letter." She ignored their surprised expressions and bolted to her room. Carefully, so it wouldn't squeak, she opened the window. She climbed out, lowering herself until her feet touched the top of the woodpile. Then she scrambled down and ran along the path through the woods.

She had never gone farther than the old stump on her own, but Alex had said there was a shortcut to the Duncan farm. Stay on the path till you get to the fork, then turn — What was it? Left or right?

She stood at the fork, trying to remember. Straight ahead went to the park. And left was back to the house, because that's the way they'd gone that first day. So the path on the right must go to the sheep farm. Hurry, hurry, she urged herself. She'd die if she got there too late.

In the distance she could hear the hounds. Was it really only two? It sounded more like a hundred! They would have started from the kill, like Mr. Pendray said, then picked up the scent from bushes the cat had brushed against. How far would he have gone? Come on, hurry!

Excitement made her run faster. I'm going on a cougar hunt! she chanted to herself. Wait'll I tell Angie!

Suddenly, a few feet ahead, two figures stepped onto the path, blocking her way. She stopped, breathing hard, fists clenched at her sides.

NINETEEN

Cougar Hunt

"I'm not going back and you can't make me!" Sam shouted. "You think you're — "

"Stop, silly!" Robyn grabbed her hand. "We're coming with you."

"We guessed what you were up to," Alex said as they ran in the direction of the hounds. "And we didn't want you to go on your own."

"Just in case," said Robyn.

"There they are." Alex pointed to the men up

ahead. "We should slow down. If they see us, they'll probably send us back."

There were four men — Matt Duncan, Joel Pendray, Uncle Lon and the contract hunter. Two of them carried guns. "I thought Mr. Pendray was only going to use a dart gun," Sam said, worried.

"That's what he's got," Alex explained. "It just looks like a regular rifle."

"What's Mr. Duncan carrying?"

"Must be the case for the darts. Remember? Mr. Pendray said he puts drugs in the darts, then loads them into the gun just before he shoots."

The scent led the baying hounds through the dense underbrush and up a fern-covered slope. "What a racket!" Sam said, covering her ears.

"I'm tired," Robyn panted. "Maybe this wasn't such a good idea."

"Too late now," her brother said. "You want to go back by yourself with a terrified cougar on the loose? What if the hounds lose the scent? No telling where he might turn up."

Sam had thought of that, too. Although if she were the cougar, she'd want to be as far away from this racket as possible. "Hey!" she exclaimed as the hounds tore across a meadow. "This is where I was the other day. This is where I saw the kittens."

"Great," said Robyn. "All we need now is to run into Cougar Mom."

"Wait!" At the edge of the meadow, Sam crouched behind a fallen tree. The others followed suit.

Up ahead, the hounds had launched into an unearthly cacophony of baying and squealing around the base of a large maple. "We've got him!" Mr. Pendray shouted. "About fifteen feet up that tree!"

"That's not all we've got," Uncle Lon said. "Poor little guy." The grim tone of his voice made the others hurry over.

"What do you think it is?" Robyn whispered, watching as the men bent over to examine something in the grass.

"I don't know." Sam's stomach was squirming. What if the cougar had killed one of the fawns?

Whatever it was, the men left it for the time being and turned their attention to the cougar.

Sam could see him clearly. He was lying on a branch, the first big one from the bottom. And he looked so relaxed. Not the least bit concerned, in spite of the racket the hounds were making. But why should he worry? There was no way the hounds could get at him.

"I thought he'd be snarling like mad," Alex said. "He actually looks bored."

"At least he doesn't look hungry," said Robyn.

From their hiding place, they watched Mr. Pendray mix the drugs and set up the dart, while the contract hunter tied the frantic hounds to a nearby tree. "Don't they ever shut up?" Alex muttered. "You'd think — "

"Sh!" Sam said. "He's getting ready to shoot."

Mr. Pendray loaded a dart into his gun, moved

to the side of the tree, took careful aim, and fired.

Ouch! Sam yelped silently as the dart landed in the cougar's rump.

At the same instant, the cougar let out a startled yowl. Before everyone's astonished eyes he sprang off the branch, made a soaring twelve-foot leap through the air, landed against the trunk of a fir tree — and clung there, limbs outstretched, gripping the bark with his sharp, curved claws.

"Wow!" Sam exclaimed. "Did you see that leap?"

"What the — " Uncle Lon spun around at the sound of her voice. "What are you kids doing here?"

"They're OK, as long as they stay well back," Mr. Pendray said firmly. "You kids got that? The cougar's got an avenue of escape, but there's no telling what might happen before those drugs kick in. Fifteen, twenty minutes, max."

The hounds were going wild. If they were loud before, it was nothing compared to the din they were unleashing now.

Sam stared at the cougar nervously. How long could he cling there? Was he starting to lose his grip? What would happen then? What if the drugs didn't work? What if he leaped from the tree and turned on them?

But he won't, she assured herself. He'll want to get away from the hounds.

But the hounds are tied up. The cougar could attack them.

But Mr. Duncan and the hunter, they've both got

real guns, just in case —

Suddenly, two things happened. In an unexpected move, the cougar twisted his body, flung himself from the tree and bounded into the bush.

At the same time, one of the hounds broke free of the rope.

"Emmy! Get back here!" the hunter yelled as he and Mr. Pendray chased after her. "Dang-blasted fool dog!"

The others followed, keeping well behind. Sam could see the cougar up ahead, making for the nearest tree. She could also see that he was tiring. Clearly, the drugs were working.

All of a sudden, the cougar stopped and whirled around. His lips drew back and he snarled, baring his fangs. The hound lunged forward. Instantly, an immense paw lashed out and struck her, raking her nose with razor-sharp claws. Yelping with pain, the bleeding dog retreated to her master's side.

"That'll teach you, Emmy girl," the hunter said. "Next time, you won't be so eager."

"Will she be all right?" Robyn asked.

The hunter patted his whimpering hound. "She'll have an awfully sore nose for awhile. Other than that, she'll be OK. Won't you, girl?"

"Guess she's feeling sheepish," said Alex.

"*Sheep*ish?" Robyn groaned. "Oh, please."

Sam turned her attention back to the cougar. His hindquarters had collapsed and his front limbs were sinking forward. His shoulders and head sagged as the drugs took effect. In a moment, the big cat lay still.

"What do you think, Sam?" Mr. Pendray asked. "Is this the fellow you saw in the park?"

Sam looked at the cougar's chestnut coat and nodded. "I'm sure of it."

The conservation officer gently rolled the cat over. "He's definitely *not* the mother. See that small circle of black fur below the belly? That shows he's a male." He took out a set of handcuffs and began to cuff the cougar, front paws crossing diagonally to hind paws.

Robyn gaped. "Are you sure he's totally anece— however you say that word?"

"You mean anesthetized? Absolutely. You can touch him if you like. As soon as we get him cuffed."

"No, thanks. I'm not getting near those claws."

"He looks dead," Sam said in a quiet voice. "Even though his eyes are open."

"I can assure you, he's very much alive." After cuffing the cougar, Mr. Pendray took some ointment from his case and carefully applied it to the cougar's eyes. "This is to keep them from drying out."

"I'd like to touch him," Sam said shyly. "Can I?"

"If you're very, very quiet. Even though he's anesthetized, he could still react to a sudden movement. Any loud noise could wake him up. That's why we cuff him."

Sam cautiously approached the cougar. Gently, she patted his head and stroked the long, silky fur on his chest. It felt warm to her touch, and soft, like

Rupert's. For a moment she kept her hand still, shivering as she felt the big cat's heartbeat. Then she asked, "Are you going to carry him back?"

"Nope, you are. With a little help," he added, laughing at her expression. "This fellow gets the limo service." He spread out a large net, and with Uncle Lon's help, rolled the cougar onto it. "Good thing you kids came along," he said. "How about helping us old guys carry the net? This cat's a big one, and heavy. I'd guess about 130 pounds. Think you can manage?"

"Sure!" As they started to head back, Sam remembered her uncle's discovery in the grass, just after the cougar was treed. "Was it a fawn you found?" she forced herself to ask.

Her uncle patted her shoulder. "No, honey." He glanced at Mr. Duncan, following behind with a small bundle in his arms. "It's a cougar kitten."

TWENTY

A Cry in the Night

"It's not fair!" Sam cried. "Why did he have to kill it?" She'd read that male cougars often killed kittens so the mother would mate again, but the knowledge didn't help.

Neither did her uncle's words. "Joel said he was likely trying to establish his own territory, and saw the male kitten as a potential threat."

"But it was so little. It didn't have a chance."

"Think of the other one, out there with its mother.

It'll be safe, now that the big male is gone."

Sam sniffed noisily. "How far gone is he?"

"Joel's taking him halfway up the island, miles from here. As soon as the drugs wear off he'll be set free."

That night, Sam couldn't sleep. She tried her usual tricks — counting sheep, counting worries, counting sounds. But she couldn't get past the one less sheep at Mr. Duncan's. She worried about the remaining cougar kitten. And the only sound she heard came from hounds, baying in her mind.

All she could think was *cougar*. The feel of the fur, the amber eyes with their round pupils, so different from Rupert's slitted ones. The sharp, curved claws. The dead kitten —

It was useless trying to sleep. She turned on the light, propped her journal against her knees and picked up where she'd left off.

The cougar didn't kill the kitten because he was bad or mean. Or the sheep, either. He did it because —

Suddenly, she heard a cry. A loud, long scream. Her heart pounded in her ears. Was someone lost in the woods?

The cry came again. No, it was too cat-like to be

human. But too human to be a cat. Unless …

If it came again, she wanted to be sure. Quickly, she ran outside. She stopped when she reached the deck, surprised to see the twins sitting on the steps, each huddled in a blanket.

"We heard it too," Robyn said quietly. She made room on the step for Sam to sit down, and spread the blanket over her shoulders.

For awhile, the only sound was water lapping the shore. Maybe that was it, Sam thought. Maybe I'll never hear it again.

But the sound did come again. A wild cry, so clear and piercing it cut the night air and made it quiver. Sam looked at her cousins. A thrill passed through them, and in one voice they whispered, *"Cougar!"*

Everyone in the house heard it, except for Uncle Lon. "Nothing could've woken me up last night," he said the next morning.

"Gee, Dad," Alex teased, "I didn't think you were so out of shape. One little walk in the woods and you're wiped out."

"*Little* walk? I'd hardly call yesterday's hunt a little walk."

"I found out why they make that sound," Sam said, opening one of her library books.

"Why aren't we surprised?" Robyn mumbled between mouthfuls of French toast. Still, she looked at Sam expectantly.

"It says here they scream to startle small game into moving, so that they'll reveal themselves and get caught. Smart, eh? Or they scream during mating season, or when they're staking ownership of territory." She put down the book and helped herself to more orange juice. "But the male's gone, so that explanation doesn't work."

"Maybe it was the mother cougar, crying for her dead kitten," said Robyn.

"Too anthropomorphic," said Alex.

"Anthropo — huh?" Robyn rolled her eyes. "Talk English, why don't you."

"For those of you with limited intelligence," he said pointedly, "it's when you give human characteristics to animals."

"How about when you give animal characteristics to humans?" Robyn shot back. "Like you. Ape brain. Worm face."

"Takes one to know one, twin sister."

Sam ignored them and went on reading. "It also says cougars hardly ever make that sound. And hardly anybody ever hears it. So we were lucky, don't you think?"

"Your parents will be sorry they missed it," said Auntie Jean.

"My parents?" Sam frowned, confused.

"They're coming tomorrow. Did you forget?"

Sam laughed. "Yeah, I guess I did!"

"Time flies when you're having fun," Alex said. "Or researching cougars. Hey, Professor?"

Sam grinned happily.

"How about picking some berries after breakfast?" Auntie Jean said. "I'll bake a blackberry pie for dinner tomorrow."

"Great idea!" Uncle Lon exclaimed. "We'll catch some salmon, get a few crabs, prove to the Torontonians we really do live off the land."

"Honestly, Dad," said Robyn.

Alex found three ice cream buckets for the berries and they set off down the driveway. "Might run into the bear today. It's that time of year."

"No way," said Sam. "Nobody would ever believe I saw a cougar plus a bear."

"Why not?" Robyn asked. "Aren't your friends as gullible as you are?"

"As I *was*."

At the end of the long driveway they turned onto the road. A short walk led to the blackberry patch. "Where did Alex get to?" Robyn grumbled. "He always manages to disappear when there's work to do."

"This isn't work," Sam said, popping a berry into her mouth. "This is fun."

"Just wait." Robyn tossed an unripe berry at Sam and laughed as it bounced off her head.

"You — " Sam picked a plump, juicy berry and threw it at her cousin, laughing when it left a purple stain on her cheek. That gave her an idea. Taking another berry she streaked her own cheeks with juice. "Do I look fierce?"

"Terrifying," said Robyn. "Now do me."

Sam had almost finished painting Robyn's face when Alex came running toward them yelling, "Cougar tracks! In the ditch, right beside the road!"

Sam and Robyn looked at each other and burst out laughing.

"It's true! I'm not kidding."

"Yeah, right." His sister grinned. "And the earth — "

" — is flat," said Sam.

"OK, don't believe me. You'll be sorry. I'm going to mix up some plaster of Paris and make a cast."

"Is that what took you so long?" said Sam. "You were drawing a cougar track in the ditch?"

"Hope you got it right," Robyn said. "Five toes, remember?"

"Four," Sam corrected.

"Right on!" said Alex. "There were four toes. You'd recognize a cougar track, wouldn't you, Professor?"

"I think so. There weren't any claw marks, were there? There shouldn't be, 'cause they pull in their claws. It's called retractable."

"All right, all right," said Alex. "Do you want to come and see, or not?"

Sam and Robyn gave each other a might-as-well-play-along look, and followed him down the road. A short distance later, he stopped and pointed at the ditch. "What do you think?"

In the damp earth, Sam saw the unmistakeable tracks of a cougar. There were four rounded toes, and no claw prints. Beneath the toes was the pad, with three distinct bumps at the base. "That's a cougar track. Definitely!"

Alex gave his sister a triumphant grin. "Was I right or was I right?"

"It must have been the one we heard last night," Sam said. "Don't you think? It really was close!"

"There's at least one print that's clear enough to make a cast," Alex said. "See?"

"Yeah … " Sam bent down and studied the area around the tracks.

"What are you looking for now?"

"I want — there!" She smiled broadly. "See this little track? Blending in with the big one? That must be the kitten. I was afraid the male cougar got both kittens, and only one was found. But now — ! That's the best going-away present ever."

Alex shook his head. "You've got cougaritis in a bad way."

"Could be worse," Sam said. "I could still have gullibility."

"Is that a word?"

"Who cares!" she giggled, and raced him back to the house for the plaster of Paris.

130

That evening, Sam was recording the events of the day when she heard a crash, followed by a scream. "You idiot! Now look what you've done!"

"You bumped into me, you stupid cow!"

"*Mom!*"

"How could you? What's Sam going to say?"

"It wasn't my fault!"

Sam ran out of her room and found the twins standing over a pile of dust and broken bits of plaster. "You didn't — ?" The question hung in the air. It couldn't be the plaster cast, could it? Not the track of the cougar!

"Yeah," Robyn sniffed. She wiped her eyes with the back of her hand and glared at her brother. "This idiot dropped it."

Sam swallowed hard, fighting back tears. "We can make another one, can't we?"

"Wish we could," said Alex. "But haven't you noticed? It's been pouring for the last two hours. All the tracks will be washed away."

Sam's face crumpled. "I don't even have a picture. We should have taken a camera … "

"Never mind." Auntie Jean came and gave her a hug. "You've got that cougar firmly engraved on your mind."

Yes, Sam thought sadly. But I did want something real. Just one little thing to keep as a souvenir.

TWENTY-ONE

Leaving

It was foggy when Sam's parents arrived. "Wouldn't you know it," her mother said. "The sun never shines out here."

The next day proved her wrong. It was clear and sunny without a breath of wind. "How about a row, Mom?" Sam suggested. "I'll give you and Dad a tour."

"Sure you don't want a hand?" Dad asked as Sam rowed into the basin.

She grinned. "Nope. I want you to see how good

I am at this. But I'll let you row back." She pointed out a great blue heron, seagulls, and sandpipers, even a couple of oyster catchers with their long red bills. Right on cue, a harbour seal popped up, and a bald eagle circled overhead.

"Ask me anything, Mom. You too, Dad. Alex said there'd be a test, but he was just kidding." Now, she caught herself wishing he *hadn't* been kidding. If she pretended to fail, she would have to stay in the Land of Fog, where night sounds wrapped around her as snugly as the quilt, and one side of the pillow was guaranteed always to be cool.

But then she wouldn't see Angie. She was looking forward to trading summer stories, and secretly hiding the loonie where Angie would least expect to find it.

"Rupert's been missing you," Mom said. "He sits at the foot of your bed and meows, wondering where you are."

"He's going to seem awfully small compared to the cougar," Sam said. "But I can't wait to have him purring on my lap."

As they entered the cove she pulled in the oars. "I call this Cougar Cove," she said proudly. "This is where it all started." The boat drifted over pink and purple starfish and waving strands of seaweed. When she heard the scrape of gravel she jumped out and tied the boat with the secure half-hitch knot Alex had taught her.

She showed her parents the arbutus where she'd

carved her name. Then she led them through the woods to the meadow.

"No sign of the cougars, now," Dad said.

Sam agreed. But they were somewhere. Maybe they were gliding through the forest on the far side of the ridge, silent as shadows. Or maybe they were hidden, mother and kitten, their coats blending with the carpet of dead leaves and tawny grasses, watching, waiting for the humans to leave the meadow.

"You weren't scared?" Mom asked. "When I think what could have happened … "

Sam clasped her mother's outstretched hand and admitted she'd been terrified. "But mostly, I felt lucky. Like when I heard the cry of the cougar that night. I felt it was a gift."

Three days later, the twins handed Sam a present. "A going-away present? For me?" She gave them a wary smile. Part of her was pleased that they'd taken the trouble to buy her something and gift-wrap it. Another part was suspicious. They'd eased up on the teasing, but were they about to play one last trick? Maybe they'd wrapped up a box of carpenter ants.

She unwrapped the present, prepared for the worst. "Nice box," she said. Then she opened it.

Inside the box was a cedar shake, varnished to a

glossy finish. And mounted on the shake was the print of her cougar. "But — I don't get it!" She ran her fingers over the white plaster, tracing the shape of the toes and the pad. "I thought — " She looked at her cousins, mystified.

"Joke," said Alex.

"Gotcha again, Gullible!" His sister grinned.

"But Robyn, you were crying!"

"We knew you wouldn't fall for just anything. Good acting, eh? Real tears and everything."

Sam's face cracked in a smile. "You guys are horrible."

Robyn gave her a hug. "And we're happy you're still our little Gullible. We wouldn't want you any other way."

TWENTY-TWO

Four Years Later

A haunting cry woke Sam in the night. She was about to go outside, hoping it would come again, when she realized she was in Toronto, not at Brackenwood Point. With the window open, she could hear the wail of a siren, but not the cry of the wilderness.

Four years later, the memory of that cry could still set her heart racing. Sleep was impossible, now. She switched on her lamp, draped a dressing gown over her shoulders and sat down at her desk. Rupert stirred from his usual spot at the foot of her bed and climbed onto her lap. She gave him the expected scratch under the chin and listened to him purr.

Cats, tracks … Rupert's paw would fit inside her thumb print. The cougar's paw was the size of her hand. She placed her palm on the plaster cast, imagining the feel of the leathery pads that muffled the sound of footsteps. She closed her eyes and pictured the cougar and kittens as she'd seen them that day, playing in the meadow, framed by the green pillars of cedar and fir.

One kitten was gone. The other would be grown now. And the cougar who had left Sam with an unforgettable memory would have a new litter. "Stay safe," Sam whispered. "Stay wild."

Her thoughts blended with the shadows. She didn't want them drifting in her mind, keeping her awake all night. She wanted to give them substance, so she could hold onto them forever.

Her new journal, labelled Number Seven, lay open in front of her. She picked up her pen, a birthday present from Robyn, and spent a moment watching the B.C. ferry cruise down the side. Then she began to write.

> *I heard the cry of a cougar once and I won't forget it. Only once. Only for a moment. There were other sounds that summer. But that's the sound I remember …*